alliance

THE BEGINNING

Sal Ardisi
Karen Nordahl
Rob Caluori

ISBN-13: 978-1718731493
ISBN-10: 1718731493

www.alliancenovel.com

This book should serve as an inspiration to the very talented artists who lie dormant. We create!

~that's all for now~

Prologue

Salvatore DePriati was born in the hills of Modonie, Sicily. For more years than anyone could count, his family had inhabited a shack of a house on the southwest side of the mountain. The place was always in a constant state of disrepair; the walls made of clay brick, blood red, with blotches everywhere. His father, also named Salvatore, labored tirelessly, filling the holes in the walls and roof that were created from the constant winds coming off the Tyrrhenian Sea.

It was a meager existence, with the family shepherding herds of sheep and goats. They worked the seasons, selling the meat when the goats became too old to produce any more milk. Every now and then, the family would make a few extra *lira* from the cheese they produced.

It was an innocent life and Sal did not know any better, having never been any further than the town of Isnello. It was not much different from the area where he lived now. It was a little place, nestled in the side of the mountain. Other than the piazza, where the townspeople gathered to do their daily business, the only other point of interest was the church. This being Italy, the Catholic faith loomed largely and the church, dedicated to St. Nicholas, was where the greater population spent their Sundays.

As Sal grew into his teen years, his father gave him more and more responsibility. Sal would drive the herd to the top of the mountain, where from Pizzo Carbonara, he could see Rome on the distant horizon. It was a sight that sparked his curiosity and the more he saw it, the more he felt the urge to leave the mountaintop. But Sal could not leave his parents, they needed him. His father was growing older and his mother struggled to keep a house in the rugged terrain. Then one day, everything changed.

Sal and his father went to Isnello to sell off some of the cheese they had made. On market day, they set up their makeshift table in the town square, displaying the cheese for sale. As they were asking people to come and buy, two men approached. They were not peasants, nor poor people looking for a deal. These two were dressed smartly, with fedora's cocked to one side. They had a swagger that spelled trouble.

As they approached the table, they picked up several pieces of the cheese. Holding the cheese close to their noses, the biggest of the two men commented, "Nice cheese. You will do well here selling this." Sal's father thanked them for their compliment and asked if they wanted to buy some. "You don't understand," the big guy said. "We aren't here to buy. You're here to pay. You want to sell, then you pay."

Sal was confused and did not understand what was going on, but his father knew exactly what was happening. These guys represented the local Don, and he had to get his tribute. They were gangsters. People who preyed on those that could not, or would not, fight back. It was protection money and everyone had to pay, including Sal's father. So, he paid and Sal learned a valuable lesson that day, but not a good one. He could see that there was a way to make money, lots of it. The only difference was, Sal would have to leave his parents, leave the mountain and he would have to leave all that he had been raised to know, behind.

That night, Sal and his father stopped at the side of the road and pitched a tent for the night. It was a long journey home and after the busy day selling cheese, they were too tired to make it back in one day. As he lay there, looking at the stars, it hit him. If he was ever going to make a move in his life, now was the time.

Stealing away into the dark night, he headed to Cefalu. It was eight miles from Isnello to Cefalu and it took Sal a few hours to get there in the dark. By morning, he was exhausted, broke, and starving. This was where his life of crime would begin.

*   *   *

As the sun broke over the horizon, Sal made his way to the seaport, where the weekly market was setting up. He was shocked when he got there because the place was unlike anything he had seen before. It was bustling with activity and the stalls were filled with everything from fish to finery. The streets were crowded with people, standing shoulder to shoulder which, for Sal, provided the perfect opportunity to snatch a few things. Amazingly, for a guy from the hilltops, he proved quite adept at stealing. In minutes he was adorned in a fancy hat, new shoes, and a smart looking shirt. He looked just like the thugs who'd come to his father's stand to extort money.

Making his way through the throngs of vendors, he looked for just the right mark. He needed to find someone, like his father, a stranger to the market. And there he was, a little old guy. He stood out from the rest of the experienced vendors, with his rickety table and dressed in rags, as if he had just come from the field. The guy was selling tomatoes. They were bright red, perfectly ripe and like the vendor, just prime for the picking.

He went up to the table and selected a couple of tomatoes, putting them to his nose and inhaling, before commenting, "Nice!"

The old man, eager for a sale, responded, "Just picked this morning. Four for one *lira*."

Sal, remembering the line from the gangster, at his father's table, parroted, "You do not understand, I am not here to buy. You are here to pay. You want to sell, you pay."

The old man looked Sal up and down and saw the fancy hat, the new shoes, the smart looking shirt and was not about to challenge him. "How much?" the old man asked.

He responded, "For you old man, just two *lira*." To Sal's surprise, the old man paid up. Sal repeated the act a few times that day, picking up quite a bit of money, but he knew his luck was not going to hold out forever and decided he had better leave Cefalu before the local Don caught up to him.

Despite his instincts on the street, Sal could not read very well. He knew he had enough money to get on a boat leaving Cefalu and he wanted to go to Rome. At the dock, he caught a steamer that was leaving and thought he was headed in the right direction. Once at sea though, Sal began to ask around about when they would berth in Rome. Much to his surprise, it turned out that the ship was not going to Rome. It was bound for New York in America. This proved a bit of a problem for Sal, because he had no papers, no passport. He had nothing. Sal was born on the mountain, which meant there was nothing to prove that he even existed.

As the steamer entered the New York harbor, Sal, who spoke very little English, had to find a way off the ship. He knew he could not leave from the gangway, because of the officials who would be meeting the boat. While the ship carried passengers, it also carried cargo. Several of the crates had loose tops and Sal went in search of a place he could hide. Finding a crate that was partially empty, he jumped inside, pulling the top down tight. As the hours passed, he finally felt one of the dock cranes take hold of the crate. It hit the pier with a thud. Then everything was quiet for a long time. Darkness fell and Sal took the chance of lifting the top. He looked around and saw that all work had stopped for the day. He was alone and now was his chance to get away. Slipping away from the docks, he headed into the city.

He found living in the city to his liking. It was a gangster's paradise and Sal soon reaped the fruits of his one-man crime wave in a big way. It was not easy at first, though, he had to do some risky things but because of his lack of fear, he soon earned the nickname, "Sally Balls." The Sally Balls thing proved to help further his criminal enterprise because it came with a reputation. And in the world of crime, reputation was everything.

Although Sal was making lots of money and living the high life, he was lonely. He was lonely for his family and he needed people around him. Over the years, he was able to reconnect with the old country, where he arranged to bring several family members to America, including a brother, Alexander, who was born after Sal left Italy.

He was also able to finally have a family of his own, having married a wonderful woman, Giana. They enjoyed many years together. Giana had gotten pregnant and bore him a son, whom they named Donald. Then tragedy struck. While giving birth to their second child, Rose, Giana died, leaving Sal without a wife and their children without a Mom. Despite the loss, Sal's family continued to grow and everyone prospered. As Sal got older, he took to living with Rose, who married a fine man, Enrico Risi. Sal loved them both dearly, they were hard workers and Rose provided him with a beautiful grandson, Frank.

The only issue for Sal was that the family had reservations about being a part of his business and he needed an heir to the throne. Sal was not willing to let his empire die and he would find a way to ensure that it continued to flourish.

CHAPTER ONE

Frank:

Oh man, I thought, as the sun, peeking through the blinds, hit my face. I pulled the covers back over my head, trying to ignore the fact that it was already ten in the morning. It was the usual time for a fifteen-year-old to get up on the weekend, but for me, it was actually late, especially since I had a game at eleven. A big game, with all the local guys who were like me, living the dream of one day being a Mickey Mantle, or at least some kind of local hero in the neighborhood, anyway.

While still dressed in my pajamas, I staggered downstairs into the kitchen, where I was not at all surprised to find Anthony and Tommy were sitting at the table, eating through a bag of jelly donuts and black and whites. My dad wasn't around much, however, the one thing that he always did was bring home a bag of pastries on Saturday mornings. My problem was that I was not always quick enough to get any of them.

I lived in a typical Italian home, where everything was decorated with floral patterns and all the furniture was covered in plastic. You know, the kind of furniture that was purchased to impress the relatives but not the kind anyone could actually sit on. I always wondered why Mom and

Dad thought things were going to get stained when they had a two-inch thick plastic covering everything. It just never made sense to me, but then again, nothing made sense in a house where things were old and rarely used. Even the kitchen was dated, it still had the appliances from when my parents bought the house in the fifties, the kind with chrome accents on everything. Today, they sell these things at premium prices and label them as art-deco. All in all, we had a nice house, pretty substantial for the time.

"Tommy, you didn't leave me anything to eat. Why don't you eat the pastries at your own house?" I asked him.

"Don't worry about that, Frank. We've got a game today and besides, you're always the last one out of bed," Tommy replied. "That's what you fucking get for being lazy."

"Yup," Anthony added, as a cloud of powdered sugar blew across the table.

"Oh, you're speaking today, Anthony?" I asked. "Nice to see you have a mouth that's used for something other than eating."

Tommy dismissed me. "Never mind him, he doesn't even know he's alive. The only thing he knows how to do best, is what you see, eat."

Anthony stopped chewing and glared at Tommy, not sure what to say, but saying a lot with his eyes. While Anthony could be a bit goofy at times, if his eyes could kill there would be a massacre at the table.

ALLIANCE

Tommy didn't seem to notice, but I'm sure he did, because he never missed anything, especially when it came to Anthony. Let's be real, how tough could Anthony look, with jelly and shit all over his mouth?

Make no mistake about him, there was something not quite right about Anthony, and it all started with the daggers he could throw when he focused in on you. To tell you the truth, it kind of freaked me out a little. But then again, that was just Anthony.

As for Tommy, well that was another story altogether. You always felt Tommy's presence, even as a teenager, he was always leading the crew, out front and aggressive. Tommy was not one of those guys to sit in the shadows and it was evident early on who he had taken after.

My mother and Tommy's father were sister and brother. Tommy's father married his high school sweetheart. They were a good-natured couple, kind, loving, and caring, the compassionate kind of people that were always there for you. One would think he would have taken after his parents. The difference here was that the gene skipped a generation and Tommy ended up emulating our grandfather, Salvatore DePriati, who stayed with us, in a bedroom on the second floor of our house.

While Grandpa was unassuming at home, in reality, he was a ruthless Sicilian, who was in the business of running numbers, gentlemen's clubs and at times, murder for hire. Really, anything that paid and paid well. The other thing about Grandpa was that he was not the kind of gangster who wore silk suits, ties, or flashy get-ups. Grandpa, or "Sally Balls," as he was known on the streets, was a unique individual. He looked like Dean Martin, dapper and debonair, and he sang like him, too.

However, Grandpa's style did not cross over in his clothes, where he always had a flair for a tacky Florida look. If you ever saw him, even in the winter in New York, you would swear he was headed to some kind of beach party. He loved shirts with palm trees and his "special occasion" one was littered with a thousand pink flamingos. You could see him coming from miles away and although his shirts were comical, his demeanor was one you feared and revered all at the same time. And trust me when I say, if you were on his shit list, you never wanted to see him coming.

"Good morning, guys," Grandpa said.

Anthony and I looked up and replied, "Good morning," in unison before returning to the details of the breakfast table.

But not Tommy, no, not Tommy. You see, Tommy worshiped Grandpa and as soon as he saw him enter the room, he jumped out of his chair, planting a kiss on each of Grandpa's cheeks, just like they do in the old country. It was like straight out of a movie and I did everything I could not to laugh because I knew what would come next and Grandpa could knock you silly with a good shot to the back of the head.

I was waiting to see if Tommy would kiss his ring, but before that could happen, Grandpa interrupted, telling Tommy, "Make sure you drop this bag off after you get done playing, same place as yesterday."

Tommy grabbed the bag, his chest all puffed out as if he had just been bestowed an Academy Award or something. The poor slob then lost his tongue and was at a loss for words, leaving Grandpa to believe that Tommy was a kid who could be trusted to do a job and keep his mouth shut in the process. What was clear to us was that Grandpa had started the grooming process and Tommy was his protégé.

Before heading out of the kitchen, Grandpa turned, saying, "And Thomas, don't disappoint me." Well, that was all it took because Anthony and I immediately knew what Tommy was thinking.

*   *   *

Tommy:

I always cringed whenever someone called me Thomas, but I knew better than to say anything to Grandpa about it. In truth, I hated it. It made me sound weak and the last thing I was ever going to be was weak. So I ignored the "Thomas" comment and grabbed the bag from Grandpa. After all, I was anxious to please him and knew full well what he expected of me. Make no mistake, I was not naive going into this. I knew what was in the bag, I always knew, but I didn't let on. I looked at Anthony and you'd think he should have known too, but he was smart enough not to say anything. Anthony understood that it was better not to know and he did everything he could to let everyone see that he wasn't the least bit interested in paying attention to me, or Grandpa.

I could never figure Anthony out. Was he happy to be here, or did he just not have anywhere else to go? And Frank looked disgusted. He couldn't hide how he felt about the relationship I had with our grandfather. Frank never took to the other side of our family and my biggest fear was that it would separate us. But for now, Grandpa's jobs were mine and I was ready and willing to dive in head first.

"You got it, Pop," I said, trying not to seem too eager. The drop yesterday went off without a hitch. Grandpa knew that too, and I was hoping that this job today meant that he trusted me to handle his affairs. There was no doubt I knew I could handle today's business. The only other concern I had at the moment was to make sure that I finished the game in enough time to take care of the drop. After all, at fifteen years old, next to being Grandpa's favorite, the only other thing that mattered was baseball. We didn't have much time before our game and while I was sitting at the table, I had a thought.

"You know, Anthony, you could come with me after the game. What do you think?" I asked.

Anthony just glared at me, again. I knew what he was thinking, or, at least, I thought I did, but I just ignored him. I knew better than to say anything to Frank. His goody-two-shoes ways always rubbed Grandpa the wrong way. Although I knew Grandpa loved Frank, I saw a certain look of disappointment on his face when he looked at him. It wasn't because Frank was stupid or anything, it was quite the opposite. People are always more disappointed when they see a capable person who's not interested in being capable. And Frank, although he was a Risi, and not a DePriati, was more than capable, he was just not interested.

We really needed to get going. "Frank, you should go get your uniform on."

I always felt like I was directing Frank. Mostly because it looked like Frank needed direction, especially with his father out of the house so much. Even so, I was never sure how much of what I told Frank actually got through to him. It didn't matter anyway, in those days it was simple and most of us were happy in the morning to just wake up and have some Parks sausages and syrup.

*   *   *

Anthony:

I watched Frank run upstairs to get changed, leaving me alone with Tommy in the kitchen. My belly ached a little from all the donuts, but I didn't care since I'd gotten the most. I saw how upset Frank looked that he didn't get one and that made me feel even better about eating them. While we were all inseparable, there was something about Frank that just did not sit well with me. He always looked at me like I was the third wheel, or that he and Tommy were better than me.

7

THE BEGINNING

Tommy and Frank were thick as thieves, even though they didn't get along sometimes, which is probably why I always felt like the odd man out. I didn't have what they had. I'm not just talking about their blood, there was a lot of money flowing through their houses. I could be in the same room as them, but I often felt like I was looking through a window at us. It wasn't that they were bad to me. My last name wasn't Risi or DePriati, I was Anthony Crespo, just a neighbor really. And it was usually easy for me to feel like they were just allowing me to be in their company.

Tommy sat across the table, just looking at me. "What?" I asked.

"Nothing, Anthony. Just nothing."

"You're staring at me all the fucking time, what the fuck?"

I never understood what Tommy thought he was accomplishing with his stare. I thought maybe he watched too many Clint Eastwood movies and figured that he could kill with just a look. And then sometimes, I thought he just stared at me with the hope of getting me angry.

I guess it was Tommy's way of not feeling like he was sitting at the table by himself, feeling like an idiot. If Tommy really knew he looked that way, you could bet he would try some macho bullshit stunt to hide the fact that he was insecure when not in the company of his cousin Frank.

Just when it looked like Tommy wanted to actually open his mouth, here came Frank, bouncing down the stairs, his hat sideways and shirt

8

untucked, to save the day for Tommy once more. I laughed at Frank's stupid look and Tommy could not help but smile too, so much for his faith in Frank.

"All right, looks like Frank is finally ready, let's get going. What do you say, hero? Are you ready to show us how your greatness extends to the field, or are you just going to take up space like you usually do?" I asked, as we stood up and grabbed our gear.

After that comment, Frank gave me a shove, knocking me sideways as he and Tommy got out the door first, letting the screen slam in my face. I took a deep breath and ran to catch up. They were talking about the line-up for today's game. Tommy was the star pitcher on our team, with an arm that could potentially rival any of the major leaguers. Rumors were that college scouts already had their eyes on him. I guess they hadn't heard him speak yet.

CHAPTER TWO

Frank:

The game was going well, but not as well as we expected. We had only played this team twice before and while they were always a challenge, we'd beaten them both times. Tommy and Anthony always said the third time's a charm, but I wasn't feeling very charmed. We had led the game through eight innings, up by one, but then in the bottom of the ninth, we were down by one. Tommy got up to bat with two outs and a runner on second, hit a shot into left field and who do you fucking think was rounding third and on his way home? You guessed right, Anthony. Even worse was he was running right past the third base coach, who was *not* waving him home. That thick-headed fuck, he was headed home and so was the throw. It wasn't on target, but close. Anthony slid home and I swear somehow he got his foot in there before the tag.

The home plate umpire, though, was out of position and didn't see it that way. Tommy had a masterpiece of a game going, with over seventeen strikeouts, but it was all dampened by one play and a bad call, because that one ump thought Anthony was out.

The entire team was yelling at the ump, but Tommy wasn't. I looked at his face, it was like he had no connection to anyone on the field, not even me. I was always looking out for Tommy, stopping him from doing something terrible. You know when you can't hear anything around you and everything is moving in slow motion? That was me looking at Tommy, who was staring at the home plate umpire. What happened at that moment was the birth of a totally different person.

*   *   *

Tommy:

I knew Anthony was safe and as much as I wanted to blame him, what was I gonna do? I had a better idea. I grabbed my bat and walked through everyone like they weren't there. The team parted like the Red Sea as I whizzed through them. The red and white of their jerseys blurred as I focused on the umpire. I hit him so many times with the bat I forgot which body part came first. Shit, I even think I heard some bones crack. Funny thing was, I never heard him scream. Like always, Frank was right there, less concerned about the umpire and more concerned about covering my ass. I don't know how the fuck Frank did it, but he always sensed the trouble I was about to create. It was like we were fucking twins at birth or something. He grabbed the blood-soaked bat from my iron grip and ran me off the field.

"What the fuck are you doing? You could kill the guy," Frank yelled, as he grabbed my shirt and dragged me behind the dugout.

"He deserved it and much more." I was screaming at the top of my lungs. I was trying to catch my breath, while Frank wanted me to lower my fucking voice. I was angry, angry at Anthony, the umpire, at Frank, at my team. I was seething. I also knew I probably should have been angry at myself, mostly regretting that I didn't kill that cock-sucking ump.

And I still had business to take care of for Pop. I told Frank, "I've got to run that errand for Pop and then maybe we can meet up after?"

He stared at me with the blood still on his hands. With a stunned look he replied, "Sure, Tommy, I'll let Anthony know," shaking his head, as he walked away, still not believing what had just taken place.

* * *

Anthony:

Frank and I walked back to the neighborhood, slowly and silently, neither one of us knew what to say. We could not believe that Tommy had snapped like that. Then again, we always had an inkling that it would not take too much for Tommy to lose it and that day he had. That poor umpire would never be the same again.

"You know, you fuck, if you had…" Frank started saying.

"If I had what, Frank?" I threw my gear bag on the sidewalk and jumped in front of him, ready for a fight. Or maybe I was looking for one, but Frank didn't bite. He was not Tommy and I knew it would take more than that to get him to jump. Ever the mediator, Frank tried to take the passive way out.

"Calm down, Anthony, you're so fucking stupid," Frank said. "What the fuck were you thinking? You run like shit and you try to score on a shallow hit like that? What did you think was gonna happen, and don't go telling me that it was just a game, because you know how we all are. It's all about winning and nothing else. Losing sucks."

"Hey, Frank, stop breaking my balls," I replied. "What do you want from me? All I was trying to do was get us a win. Your cousin didn't have to beat the ump like he did."

"You kidding? You're lucky it wasn't you, too. Then they would be carting you off to the hospital, along with the umpire."

CHAPTER THREE

Anthony:

After Frank left me, and Tommy was off doing what Grandpa had commanded him to do, I was left alone. While I was walking home, I did a little daydreaming, realizing that my house was much different from Tommy and Frank's. Their house was full and I was an only child, but other things were different too.

For an Italian family, we weren't that tight. There were no Sunday dinners, the innocent squabbling among family members was absent and most of all, the traditions, as a whole, seemed non-existent, save for the visiting to other people's homes, like Frank's. It was just plain unusual because the other families were close-knit and stuck together. I felt like a vagrant in my home.

My father wasn't around that much, kind of like Frank's. But what was different was that my mother wasn't around much either. It was a lonely existence and for a young teenager, it was a tough position to be in. I really had no one to talk to, no one to share my day-to-day experiences with. It was a lonely life.

ALLIANCE

I still couldn't believe what I'd seen today, but I was not surprised. I knew what Tommy was becoming and that it was leading up to moments like what happened on the field. His temper got the better of him, more so, each day. Even though he didn't blame me, deep down, I knew that he and Frank believed it was my fault. That would mean I would be excluded from something else, further down the road.

I made it home and it was just like I'd left it. The other thing I always noticed about my house was just how quiet it was. You know, when you have that feeling that nobody even knows you exist, that you are invisible, like part of the wallpaper. Always there, but nobody really sees you. And if that was not bad enough, I felt like I did not have an identity either. In fact, I didn't even like my last name. That's probably pretty odd to hear, right? What did it matter anyway? My parents didn't care. Frank didn't care. And I know Tommy didn't care.

I was in my room resting when my father came to the door.

"Anthony, what are you doing?" Dad asked from the hall. "Why are you in the room with the lights off?" He then cracked open my bedroom door and flipped on the light switch.

"No reason," I replied.

Taking a look around, he then zeroed in on my hands. "What's that on your hands? Are you bleeding? That's blood, isn't it?"

I just stared at my father. He didn't care that I played baseball. Hell, he probably didn't even know that I played. How was I going to answer him? What was I going to say? Tommy bashed an umpire's brains out at a game, cause I'm slow as shit? Well, I didn't have to tell him anything as he just walked away, not even waiting for my response. And there I was, alone again. It's probably why I was at Frank's a lot, not that they paid attention to me more than anyone else, but at least there were people around.

Maybe I should go wash my hands. I'm really nothing like Tommy, but for a minute, with that blood on my hands, I felt alive, like its presence gave me some special power over things. I could feel the bat in my hands, I could feel the bones break and hear the crack of the skull. I was in awe of what happened and how easy Tommy made it look. I think that, deep down inside, I wished it was me that was holding the bat, but in reality, I didn't have Tommy's nerve to do what he did in broad daylight. That nerve was the difference between all of us.

*   *   *

Tommy:

I wasn't at all surprised to find the police at my house, after all, I had just bashed the brains out of the umpire and there was no reason to believe I was not going to be visited by the cops. I could see them as I walked up the sidewalk from the street. I picked up the pace, trying to get to the house before the police could get to my Mom. Shit, I didn't even bother to wash the blood off my hands. I was too late. There they were, standing in the doorway, with my mother already in full denial. I could see the anguish on her face, shaking her head thinking, "No, not my son."

Even though I knew it was inevitable that the cops were going to be on to me, I wasn't going to deliver myself to them like a gift-wrapped present. So, I went around to the back of Frankie's house, where I saw him sitting at the kitchen table. He had not washed the blood off his hands either. We must have been the two stupidest mother-fuckers in the world. Frank jumped out of his chair, angry. "What the hell are you doing? I'm gonna have to hide you. They came here first."

Of course, like always, I had to calm him down. The kid was smart, but he shied away from trouble at all costs. That was probably what created the space between him and Grandpa in the first place. You couldn't do what I was doing, with fear in your mind. Fear can be a great motivator, but it was holding Frank back from being so much more. Frank could really fit into this life if he would just let go of the delusion that people were good. People are not good. They are evil and those who are the evilest usually prevail. It was just that simple, but Frank might never learn this and one day it might lead to his undoing.

It was up to me to be the leader once again. I let Frank know just what was going to happen. "I'm going to go upstairs to your room and hide and you're gonna wash the blood off your hands, Frank," I demanded.

Without a word, Frank just nodded and off he went.

After he was gone I sat there and realized that unlike Frank and Anthony, I had a pretty good relationship with my father. That was until I started working for Grandpa. My father ran a construction business, a legit one, believe it or not. He wanted nothing to do with Grandpa's line of work. Donald DePriati was tough, he didn't need to be a "made" man, to be feared. He didn't need any part of his father's business to be respected.

As I got closer to Grandpa, I could feel my relationship with my Dad straining. It had no effect on my mother and me, though. My mother was the sweetest person you could ever meet. Like all Italian mothers, though, she sometimes showed her love through the use of a wooden spoon. It was not designed to hurt you, just to send a message that she wanted you to stay on the straight and narrow.

I remember coming home drunk one time and knowing I reeked of alcohol. I tried showering, to rinse off the smell but, it didn't take much for her to figure out what was going on. All it took was one glance. My mother was smart and you could not pull the wool over her eyes. It was like she could read my mind, or had a crystal ball because she knew. My mother always knew.

While I was in the shower, I saw her arm reach in and next thing I knew, the water went cold and she was punching me in the face. I was naked, drunk, and cold. I screamed, "Mom, get out! I'm not dressed!"

She yelled back, "Nevermind that! I made that body and I can break it!" All the humiliation in the world never stopped me, though. I still drank. It was just the nature of things. I would always be thick-headed and I would always do whatever I wanted.

In truth, I deserved all the beatings. My mother cared about everyone and everything, always putting others first, even before herself. It was through her tough discipline that she showed me she loved me. My Mom and I were tight and I always felt like I was her favorite, especially since my brothers were so much older and already out of the house.

Believe it or not, I had a high IQ. I did well in school when I applied myself. Some would say I could be great at anything, but I was fascinated by the power that came along with the type of work Grandpa was doing. Running numbers between the establishments he owned, gave me a sense of ownership. I just had to make sure the money got to the right person at the right time and I was good at that.

However, what I was not good at was I wasn't supposed to draw attention to myself. That was Cardinal Rule Number One. The stunt I pulled that afternoon didn't go unnoticed. In fact, the next day the headline in the fucking paper read, 'DePriati Strikes Out Seventeen in Losing Effort; Loses Cool, Clubs Umpire.'

To think that was going to escape Grandpa's radar was a pipe dream and I knew the wrath of his anger would be something that I would have to face sooner or later. What I feared more than that was that he might reject me forever. Where would I go from there?

CHAPTER FOUR

Frank:

As I was washing the blood off my hands in the kitchen sink, I heard Tommy go up the steps, but he never made it to my room. All I heard, was Grandpa yelling at Tommy, "You're gonna bring attention to me? Then, I'm gonna give you some attention." Then the bedroom door closed and I only imagined the pain Tommy was feeling, as Grandpa beat the crap out of him.

I finally heard Grandpa's door open and knew it was safe to go upstairs. I laughed for a second, nervously caught off guard. I could not believe what I was seeing. There was Tommy in my room, smiling at me, an egg on his forehead, and a shiner on his eye. He had a bottle of Jack in his right hand. Tommy had just taken a beating for what he'd done wrong, but instead of crying like most of us would have, he just looked at me, smirking and took a swig from the bottle. To say I was a little scared would be a lie because after a beating from Grandpa, you did not laugh, smile, or smirk. The only thing you did was hurt, lick your wounds, and hope it would never happen again.

THE BEGINNING

Tommy went home just before dinner and I found myself sitting at the table with Grandpa while Mom was preparing the meal. "Were you with him today?" Grandpa leaned in and asked me.

"How could I not be? We were playing baseball," I answered, probably a little too sarcastically, but it came out of my mouth too quickly to stop.

"So, you let him beat the umpire with that bat, knowing what trouble that could have caused, you little shit?" Grandpa hissed at me, trying not to let Mom hear the anger in his voice.

"I didn't let him do anything. How could I stop him, if I didn't know what he was going to do in the first place?" Now I was getting angry, but still trying not to piss Grandpa off any more than he already was. I knew what was coming next. It was the recruitment speech. The one that always came when Grandpa thought he could exploit the moment, leaving me feeling guilty for not being the brains of the operation and ensuring that these kinds of things did not happen.

"You never pay attention to anything, Frank. You could be just as useful as your cousin," Grandpa said.

"Useful?" I interrupted. Now I'm really pissed. Grandpa knew nothing about me. We lived in the same house and yet it felt like we were worlds apart.

"Yeah, useful, like, have a purpose," he said, cryptically. He thought I knew what he was talking about and even though I did know, I wasn't going to let on. Except, I could not keep my big mouth shut.

"A purpose to do what? The things you do?" I was raising my voice and Mom turned her head slightly towards me, suddenly taking interest in this little argument between Grandpa and me. I knew it was not wise to get her involved, so I sat back in my chair and tried to calm down.

But, even as I was trying to defuse the situation, Grandpa's face was getting redder and he was heating up. "The things I do? See Frankie, that's your problem, you've got a smart mouth, but no guts. I don't see you on my side of things, going forward."

At first, I couldn't figure out what he meant by that comment. Was it because Grandpa had no faith in me? All because I wouldn't take part in his "business"? I knew Grandpa wanted me to work with Tommy, but I wanted nothing to do with that life. For him to say I wasn't on his side made no sense.

Thankfully, Mom dropped a plate of fried meatballs in between us so I could concentrate on the food. If she would've just quickly strained the spaghetti, I could have kept my eyes on my bowl rather than look at Grandpa. Lord knows there was a lot I could say, but I knew that the smarter play was to keep my mouth shut.

THE BEGINNING

*   *   *

Tommy:

Usually, after taking a beating like that, the only way I could make myself feel better was to play records in my room. But I wasn't able to do that this time, because my mother came to me to talk about the police and why they'd come to the house. I should have known there was no way to get past what happened and it was time to face the music. The only problem was that I would have preferred to have dealt with the cops, rather than with my Mom. Mostly because I didn't want to upset her and I knew bringing the cops to her front door was one of the worst things I could do to her.

"Tommy, what are you doing to yourself and what the heck happened to your face?" Mom asked, looking me over. She looked confused, concerned, and hopeless all at once. I wanted to take it all away and calm her down. Usually, she couldn't stay mad at me very long, but I was probably pushing the limits of that nowadays and it was going to take a lot to ease her fears that I was taking a turn for the worst.

"Don't worry about it Mom, things just got out of hand at the ball field… something just happened and it was no big deal."

"Something happened? The police came here and said you took a baseball bat to the head of one of the umpires. That's not just something and it certainly is a big deal." Mom was raising her voice, which she rarely did and that's how I knew she was pissed.

24

Unfortunately, I didn't always control myself in the face of confrontation, even when it was towards my Mom.

"I know Mom, but I only hit him only a couple of times. And he deserved it," I yelled at her, startling even myself.

Mom fumbled for words. "What? Why are you talking like this? Have you been hanging out with Grandpa? It has to be that because I didn't raise you to be a gangster. Who goes and beats up innocent people who are just trying to do their jobs? This has to be your Grandfather's doing. Nobody else can influence you like this."

"No," I answered abruptly.

"No? No, you say? Then what's this?" Mom asks as she pulls out a wad of cash from her pocket. "I found this under your mattress. Do you take me for a fool Thomas? You don't think I know what goes on with your Grandfather's business?"

"Is that the only thing you found?" I cut in, trying to stop her ranting before the conversation got to a place where I could not answer her.

"That's the only thing I paid attention to," she replied tactfully. "Let's get back to this money, where is it from?"

"Well, I've been saving up," I lied, as I was grasping at anything that was going to get her to stop looking at me like I had just robbed the First National Bank. She knew it was a lie, too, and I was sinking fast.

"Saving up? That's more money than your father makes in a month," she continued. I could see that Mom was not going to let this go and had much more to say than I'd anticipated and none of it was good.

"What do you want from me, Mom? I'm just trying to make a living."

"A living... a living? You're fifteen-years-old, you should be going to school, playing ball and hanging around with your friends."

"That's boring, Mom. I'd rather make money. We need money to live, don't we?"

"It's not like you were sharing it with us."

"I was going to," I lied, again.

"From here on in, you'll no longer work for your Grandfather. If you do, I'll..." and then Mom stopped talking suddenly and before I knew it, she dropped to the floor, barely missing hitting her head on my dresser. I yelled for my father and he ran upstairs. He scooped Mom up and took her into their bedroom.

From that day forward, Mom was never quite the same again. She was in and out of the hospital. They ran tests for weeks and she wasn't getting better. Instead, she got progressively worse. The doctors finally told us what we did not want to hear and that was that she had cancer. I didn't even know what the fuck that was but was hoping I could beat it with a bat, kill it before it killed her.

ALLIANCE

From that point on, my father did everything to try to make the situation better. He tried to learn about this cancer stuff. What was it? They called it the silent killer. One day you were fine and the next day they were telling you to get your affairs in order. It was all a shock because this was my mother and I could not help but feel guilty. I kept thinking I did this to her. That what I had done had triggered this thing, this cancer. Now it was going to kill her and it was all my fault.

The doctors tried everything, too, including the experimental stuff. But in the end, all it did was make her sicker, weaker, a shell of her former self. At one point, she could barely speak. She tried to be strong, but you could see the desperation in her eyes. She wanted to tell me that everything would be all right and that I was not to blame. Her eyes, it was her eyes that spoke to me. It was the love for her son that I could see. It was her way of letting me know that no matter what happened, I was always her son and she would always love me, no matter what.

That was not enough for me. I was angry all the time and it didn't help that my father was not talking to me, because of Grandpa. Now with Mom sick, he couldn't even look at me. He spent time consoling the rest of the family, trying to make my brothers feel better, but not me. There was that blame again. I could see it. He blamed me for what happened.

At one point, during all that, I couldn't recognize my mother. I would go into her bedroom and she would just stare at me. She ended up dying in the hospital, still trying to battle her way through the cancer.

THE BEGINNING

She wouldn't even let me see her in the final moments of her life. I never got to say goodbye. Is there anything worse than that?

CHAPTER
FIVE

Frank:

After Tommy's mother died, things were never the same again. My cousin became unrecognizable. Don't get me wrong, it bothered all of us, but for him, it was like a light went out, or like a door closed to a room, never to be opened again. He became destructive, with no feelings. He was completely wild, with an uncontrollable temper. It may have all been part of the change he was undergoing but it was clear that the kinds of things he was doing could lead to his demise.

Tommy drank more and more and then he started using drugs. It set him apart from the rest of us because it was not a line that we were prepared to cross. The alcohol and the drugs, combined with the work he was doing for Grandpa, well… you get the picture. Tommy was lost.

Our lives over the next several years were spent going to concerts, hanging out and drinking. And when there was alcohol involved, at some point, Tommy would break. One thing was certain, he would get wasted and get either violent or he would be so emotional that you knew, even though his mother was gone, she was always right there. And not necessarily in a good way.

It was difficult being the voice of reason for him when I didn't even understand him myself. As much as I hated to admit it, I could not help Tommy and he sure as hell was not going to help himself.

* * *

Anthony:

While I had a feeling about what was going on between Frank and Tommy, I knew that they did not need me. But over time, all of that would change. There was no doubt that I felt bad about Tommy's mother passing away. She was a great person and like a Mom to me, as well.

After her death, if Frank wasn't babysitting Tommy, I was. We got a lot closer after his mother's death but I questioned whether or not he wanted me around because he was afraid to be alone, or if he really wanted me there. Tommy seemed to want my company, but he always kept me at arm's length. I was not privileged to know what he was doing for his Grandfather and he never wanted me to help him out with any of the "errands" he was doing. Make no mistake, his Grandfather kept him plenty busy and didn't give two shits what Frank and I thought it was doing to Tommy.

Tragedy never lives alone and shortly after Tommy's Mom died, it struck my home too. It was not as dramatic, with my father passing away. My father died more suddenly from a massive heart attack that occurred as he was mowing the lawn one afternoon. But, you wanna know the real shitty part? There wasn't even a whisper from either Tommy or Frank about it. That's how it was for me. What was I to expect though? They barely knew my father. What they failed to realize is that it was me who needed the support. While I thought Frank and Tommy were my best friends, often they acted like they did not even know me.

Even though I had no real relationship with him, he was still my Dad. So, to have my friends around me and not have them care was a fate worse than death. I would never forget that Tommy and Frank were not there for me.

CHAPTER SIX

Tommy:

After Anthony's Dad died, we all grew up really fast. Frank became more serious, actually studying in school. Anthony, well Anthony was the same dumbass he'd always been, but we just could not leave him out of the group. So, we still hung out through our teenage years until things started to change as adults.

Believe it or not, I was the first one to get engaged. We were all in our early twenties, but because of what I was doing, I was a bit worldlier than the two of them. What the fuck was I thinking? Frank was dating Mary and Anthony was messing around with some girl whose name I didn't even know.

With the business I was in, I didn't have a lot of time for a relationship and I don't even know why I tried, I was way too young. But then again, Samantha was a horse of another color and it was hard to ignore her.

Samantha, or Sam as I liked to call her, was gorgeous. She had blonde hair and blue eyes and a body that didn't quit. In the beginning, she was cool. We were both into heavy metal music and we fucked like rabbits. But regardless of the physical bliss, it seemed like she was always complaining. I think it was all about the money. I spoiled her way too much and she was never satisfied.

By then I was running most of Grandpa's businesses and yeah, I was wearing those tacky floral shirts typically reserved for retired old men living in Boca. Along with the money came the drinking and as it turned out, Sam could drink me under the table. What should I have expected, she was Irish for fuck's sake.

"Samantha, you just gonna sit there and drink all night, or you gonna give me a little?"

"Oh… so, you're talking to me now?" she snipped.

"Well, who the fuck else am I gonna be talking to? I don't see anyone else behind you."

"You know, Thomas, you would have gotten some if you'd come home last night, on time."

"What? You know one day you're…" I was so pissed right now. Sam had such a sharp tongue and knew that calling me Thomas was the last thing she should ever do. She couldn't shut her mouth and kept coming at me.

"Oh, cut your shit, Tommy. This whole thing is just a sham, you couldn't give a shit about me."

"Really? Then I guess I should cut off the money too because if you could say that, I guess it means you don't give a shit about me either."

And this was the problem between Sam and me. She could be all peaches and cream one day and the next, Sam was the biggest bitch I ever met. Yeah, I was to blame for some of it, but she knew that I hated to be called Thomas and only did it to get under my skin. I had little self-control as it was and when Sam called me Thomas, well, it was difficult not to want to whack her right then and there.

*   *   *

Samantha:

Tommy could be a real prick, with his wild mood swings and his propensity to turn violent at the drop of a hat. But for all that, I knew him as a different guy. I knew that there was more to him than that tough guy Mafioso persona he displayed on the street, or when he was with his crew. Most of all, I was keenly aware Tommy was someone whose pain was greater than he would ever let on. He had demons and they affected how he loved and how he lived.

When we first met, Tommy took me to one of his clubs. That first night he introduced me as his future wife. It completely blew me away. I could see there was a hint of romance to him, but marriage on the first date was not something I wanted to buy into. And don't get me wrong, I liked the money, the gifts and how Tommy treated me like a queen. It kept me from having to do what I'd done in my "past life," something

I wouldn't want to tell my kids about if I ever had them. This was where Tommy was an evil bastard because he used what I used to be to control me. Yeah, it was always about the money. And when it wasn't about the money, it was about his family. Especially Frank, because he was always on the other side of the tracks. I never saw why Tommy liked him so much.

For me, I could take Frank just as much as I could leave him. There was something about Frank that wasn't quite right. I think it was because he came off as too nice a guy and I didn't buy it. When it came to the streets, Tommy was a genius and Frank, well, he didn't have the same experience. But in some respects, I also felt like Frank was playing dumb when it came to Tommy's business. He made it plainly clear that he wanted no part of that life and that is probably one of the main reasons why I did not trust him, no matter how Tommy felt.

*   *   *

Frank:

I knew Samantha had an inner dislike for me. She probably didn't like Anthony either and wasn't going to like the fact that we had both decided to become cops. The test was coming up and Anthony and I were preparing for it together.

I bet if Anthony didn't decide to be a cop, he would have joined Tommy in his line of business. The only difference was that Anthony was not built to play second fiddle to Tommy. Being a cop was the only other thing that would give him a safe outlet to have power, which it seemed like he was after more and more nowadays.

Crazy as it sounds, for me, it was not so much about getting away from Tommy and Grandpa, as it was to have a steady paycheck and a job with a future. I did not want to look over my shoulder every day and being a cop allowed me to have a measure of respect, without having to kill anyone.

We took the test and it seemed to go well. I'm not sure how Anthony did on it, but he didn't complain that it was too hard. I got my results in the mail and headed over to Anthony's to show him. He must have gotten his, too.

"Did you get your test results back, Frank?" Anthony asked me as soon as I walked up to his porch. He was holding the same envelope as me.

"Yeah, and...?"

"I got an eighty-five. Where are you on the list? I'm number three, what about you?" Anthony replied. I ripped open my results and snickered towards Anthony.

"I'm number two, and once again, in front of you."

"So did you tell anybody about this? Including your cousin?" Anthony asked, ignoring my jab about the score.

"No. I was trying to figure out how to bring it up," I replied.

"You're going to be a cop for Christ's sake, Frank. You're not going to be able to hide it. Soon, you're going to have to tell people."

Anthony was right and I knew it. I also knew there was no way I was going to be able to convince Tommy or Grandpa for that matter, that this was what I needed to do. Let's be honest here, I was supposed to be a crook, a gangster, someone who would carry on the legacy of the family. The only difference was that I did not want any part of that and while I loved Tommy like a brother, I did not want to sit inside a jail cell beside him.

As we were sitting in front of Anthony's house, I was looking at him and thinking to myself it was the most confident I had ever seen him. He had developed his own style and was doing his hair in such a way that actually looked human. Hell, he was even talking differently. The most peculiar thing he said to me, and I tried not to pay it any mind, was that he wanted to change his last name. You see, Crespo never sat well with him. It was synonymous with failure in his mind. Maybe there was something else to it as well. I never saw anything wrong with his last name, so his desire to be someone else may have been the reason why he was so hell-bent on changing it.

But getting back to when I thought I should let other people know I was going to be a cop. That was another story altogether. It was a delicate subject for sure and one I just was not ready to do yet.

Anthony was staring at me, waiting for a response.

"Listen, Anthony, I'm gonna tell Tommy when the time's right. Obviously, I can't keep doing what I'm doing, swinging a hammer isn't gonna cut it much longer. I need, no, I want, to be something better and I am thinking that being a cop is going to provide the path for that. Plus, the money isn't bad either."

"You don't think there's gonna be any competition with what we're trying to do? I don't got nothing going on right now, this is all I got. I don't even want to be a local cop and I was thinking of going federal," Anthony said.

"You? In the FBI? Are you fucking kidding me? I think Tommy's gonna freak out just to know we're gonna be cops in this city. Now you're talking about becoming a federal agent? I think you have a few screws loose in that head of yours. Either that or all the gel you've plastered on your hair has poisoned your brain."

For a brief second, I watched Anthony's face drop, almost as if he'd reverted back to when we were kids, like he'd fallen off the top of a tree and I was the one who'd pushed him. I didn't think he couldn't do it, I just didn't understand why. I guess becoming an FBI agent would be another way for him to get away from all he knew about himself. Or, maybe, like when we were kids, it was another way for him to show that he measured up to us, or that he was better than us.

CHAPTER SEVEN

Tommy:

I had just gotten home from a Florida trip that needed to be taken. It was one of those things that took me away from home again and lately, that seemed to be happening more and more. The Florida business was expanding and with the growth there were problems. Problems had to be handled and could only be handled by me, personally.

I really had to get someone else to do the dirty work of this business, though. I also knew that there was no one else I could trust right then and like they say, if you want something done right, you have to do it yourself. Just at what cost?

"Samantha, ya home? Samantha?"

I saw her car out front, so I knew she was home. What the fuck? Where was she? The lights were out in the living room but as I walked further into the house, I heard noises. They were coming from upstairs. As I climbed the steps to the second floor, I saw the bedroom door was open a bit and a yellow glow was coming from the room. I walked in and there she was, on all fours on the bed and you wouldn't fucking believe who was behind her- one of my line cooks, Dante. Not a doctor, not a lawyer, or a fucking astronaut, but a guy I had cooking hamburgers in the basement of the bar. Basically, a bum!

Believe it or not, I had to laugh, because he was so focused, but after seeing me, Dante backed out of her so fast that his dick probably got whiplash. I could see semen running down her leg, so that fucker even came in her. And what was worse, what added insult to injury, was that he was built like a thimble. I mean there was nothing to the guy. My thumb was bigger than his dick. What in the world could she have seen in him?

"Samantha, what the fuck are you doing?" I asked her, incredulous at what I had just witnessed. This was the girl I was going to marry. This was the girl I stood up at the bar and passed off as the future Mrs. DePriati. What the fuck was I thinking?

"Uh, I don't know," Sam answered my question, as she grabbed the sheet, you know like they do in the movies to cover themselves. Amazingly, she tried to look all innocent, as if what had happened there was not her fault.

Samantha stammered, "He, uh, forced himself on me. He came in here and forced me. I swear Tommy. I would never..."

To my complete surprise, Dante found his voice and interrupted Sam, saying, "I swear Don Tomas, I didn't force myself on her. It was all her idea." Dante continued to stammer something indistinguishable as he was trying to cover himself up. He was running around the room looking for his clothes. There was a fear in his eyes that he couldn't hide, it was the look I had often seen, just before I put the lights out on someone.

After Dante swore he did not force her, Samantha stood up and put her hands on her naked hips. After dropping the sheet she was using to cover herself, she began screaming at the top of her lungs. "I told *you* to come here every Friday night for the last few months, you fuck? No, you didn't force me, you were just dumb enough to get us caught."

How stupid could you get? She was so slighted by him saying it was her idea that she gave the whole thing up in a second, out of ego. I was very proud of myself. You would think I would have shot them both right then and there but I really found the whole thing quite comical. Don't get me wrong, they were gonna pay, just not that particular night, though.

I have to admit, she looked as hot as hell standing there all naked and sweaty. She was very curvy and had a full body with a heart-shaped ass. I thought about giving it to her one last time, but Dante had polluted her and even I'm not that crazy.

So, I just walked out. That really was the smart thing to do, that way there was no shit going on at the house that may have made the cops come. Besides, it was going to give me great pleasure to know that Sam and Dante would be looking over their shoulders everyday.

THE BEGINNING

*   *   *

Samantha:

Fuck! I can't fucking believe I got caught. And with fucking Dante, that asshole? I couldn't have been with Ramone or Jared, or one of the hotter ones? No, it had to be Dante. If I was gonna get caught, I would have at least liked it to have been with someone who would have made Tommy jealous.

Who the hell was I kidding? I should have been thanking my lucky stars I was alive and not just alive, but in one piece, too. I'd seen Tommy nearly kill people for a lot less than this. When he gets angry, it's vicious. The crazy thing was, the more Tommy was violent the more it turned me on. In a way, I must be as sick as him, clearly so, because I tempted fate by sleeping with Dante.

But what was really strange about that night was that Tommy didn't get angry. He didn't yell or throw a fit. He just walked away. But I did catch a glimpse of something frightening. It almost looked like he was smiling, yet not quite a smile, it was more like a smirk. If there was ever a time when I should be scared of what he might do, that look guaranteed that I better grow eyes in the back of my head.

CHAPTER EIGHT

Tommy:

Benny Costa was one of the coldest hit-men on the East Coast. He was one of those guys that actually liked to kill people and relished it like a sport. It was not just the killing. Benny liked to take his time, make the guy feel every bone-crunching element of the act and it did not matter what he used to get the deed done. He could kill you with a feather, just as effectively as putting a gun to your head and pulling the trigger. He was just that ruthless.

Benny was also a free agent and I got the word out that I wanted to meet with him now that he was back in New York. It was time for me to get a guy like Benny on my crew and like I said before, I needed some help in handling some of the "details," arising from the daily business. Plus, some of those things that were not part of the business as well.

I was in the back of the bar and heard a voice coming from the front, "Benny Costa, here to see Mr. DePriati. He's expecting me." It was Benny all right and like a true professional, he was as prompt as ever. The barmaid sent Benny over to me and I gave him the once-over. He was known to have a high body count and definitely looked the part of a stone-cold killer. He was rail-thin tall and had no color in his face. He looked like the Pale Rider. It was a look that shouted death, like the grim reaper or some shit like that. For a second, he even had me wondering. To say Benny was a presence would be an understatement. Truth be told, part of me wasn't sure about bringing anyone else on, keep fewer hands in the pot, if you know what I mean.

But the bigger you get, the more help you are going to need and Benny was just the kind of help I needed. It was time for me to get a number one hammer around here, other than myself. And he was it.

"Mr. DePriati." Benny shook my hand with a firm grip that just screamed confidence. If he was afraid of me it was not evident in his handshake. It was a good way to judge a man. No sweat, no pussy grip. Pure business, just the way I liked it.

"Benny Costa, nice to meet ya," I said.

"Pleasure's all mine. Your Grandfather is a gem and we used to call him 'Sally Balls.' He's quite the businessman."

Aside from the niceties, and a little respect for my Grandfather, Benny's conversation was very short. From what I already knew, Benny was never the kind of guy that said much anyway. Hey, he was hired for action, not words. So all I had to ask him was, "How much?" After a couple of nods and some sign language, we arrived at a number. See, there were reasons I could use a guy like Benny. He was a very loyal person and would never turn on the people who showed him respect. He killed for a living... just never his employers.

"So when you want me to start?" he asked. It was really a rhetorical question since he was already a part of my crew from the minute he stepped into the bar, but I liked he was being respectful.

I told him, "It's not when, it's with whom."

I had a short list for now and there was a shining star that deserved top billing and all the attention that Benny was going to provide.

"You got a list?" Benny wondered, like he was reading my mind. So, I chuckled as Dante was coming up from the basement. The timing couldn't have been better. We both watched Dante walk across the bar. Benny was sizing him up and I was thirsty for blood.

After I filled Benny in on the details, he just looked at me puzzled. It was because he knew of my reputation and figured that this guy would be in the ground already, or at least fired.

"Nope, I didn't fire him. Not yet, anyway. I wanted him good and comfortable. Fortunately, jobs are scarce, so he can't quit either and it's just better business to have let him and Samantha be for a while," I told Benny.

He nodded, understanding the logic, even though I knew if it was him that this had happened to, there would be two missing persons on the police blotter.

I was being smart for once. I was thinking, should I do it right now or give Benny some time to set up shop? This is a unique hitman, whose weapon of choice was known to be a large wrench. Can you imagine someone using a wrench on a job like this? Like I said, Benny liked to kill and kill slowly. I was going to enjoy watching him work.

CHAPTER
NINE

Frank:

Tommy was all set up. He had the rackets, drugs, women, and the bar, while I was just trying to make a living. Anyone will tell you, growing up in the 80's that there wasn't a lot out there. The competition was great and I didn't do what Tommy did, so money couldn't come that easily, plus I didn't have much of an education. I used my hands and I had skills as a builder. I did that while I waited to be called for the police department.

I'd been with Mary for a year or so and wasn't even thinking about getting married. It surprised me that Tommy was engaged because marriage was the furthest thing from *my* mind. I was looking to get a steady job with the police before I did anything more permanent. Of course, as luck would have it, well, my luck anyway, Mary got pregnant and in those days, we still did the right thing, when those kinds of things happened.

"You're pregnant? Are you sure?" I asked Mary. "I really can't believe it, I mean…" I didn't know what to say. On one hand, I was in denial, yet on the other hand, I was kind of excited. I'd always wanted to be a father, just perhaps not this soon. I wasn't ready, not that anyone is ever ready. I had so much more to accomplish before I could focus on raising a child.

"Well, believe it and I didn't do it by myself," Mary said. "I'm not trying to trap you, Frank. Things just happened."

I could tell she wasn't expecting my reaction and, of course, I didn't say the right thing. I should have been more supportive, but a gut reaction is just that. "You realize I don't even make a good enough living to support a family right now? I'm barely scraping by. I don't know how the heck we'll be able to make this work."

"I'm not getting an abortion Frank, if that's what you're thinking."

"No, I wasn't thinking that." Okay, maybe I did think about it for a split second, but I knew that wasn't a decision I wanted to be responsible for making. I was glad when she said she wasn't considering it.

Mary interrupted my thoughts. "How'd you do on the police test?"

"I did well. I'll probably get hired. Did you tell your parents about the baby yet?"

"No, I wanted to tell you, so you can be prepared when you see my Dad coming for you." Mary laughed a little as she said that.

"Well, they like me, no?" I asked.

Mary chuckled. I don't know how she thought any of this could be funny. "Well, they *did* like you."

*   *   *

Tommy:

Can you believe this shit? Frank gets Mary pregnant and here I am about to settle the score with the "Hamburglar." That's a great name, right? Fucking Benny named him. A killer with a sense of humor, too? Who knew?

Dante was cleaning up the kitchen for the night, unaware that he was still at the top of my shit list. He was alone so I knew the time was right to set Benny loose and once and for all take care of Dante and his wandering dick.

"Benny, he's downstairs and the place is closed up, do what you do best."

Benny didn't say anything. He simply gave me a look and went downstairs. I stayed upstairs to wrap up some business and have a nightcap. A few minutes later, I heard screaming, not exactly what I was expecting, but I trusted Benny, he was a professional. Curiosity got the best of me, so I decided to head downstairs and see with my own eyes the masterpiece that was Benny Costa at work.

The basement in the bar was half a dungeon, the other half a kitchen. This was the first time I even considered whacking someone in any of my businesses, especially this one. The place was called Ron's. It was where it all started for me and it is where we all partied while I do this thing I do. I had two guys work the front for me: Seamus and Neal. They were left over from when my Grandfather owned it and worked many hours between the two of them. Ron's was a beautiful place, from the walls that were decorated with antiques, to the impressive carved wooden bar. The place was timeless. It didn't matter what time of the year it was, when you added color, it had the warmth and feel of Christmas.

Believe me, what was about to happen in the basement was a far cry from any holiday. Now that I think about it, I should have taken him across the street to my business associate, Colum, better known as "Flatts."

Flatts ran an Irish Bar across the street called "The Saloon." Obviously, I wasn't gonna drag Dante over there to kill him. Maybe I'll dump the body in Flatts' car. It has been a while since I fucked with him. Besides, I owed him for the last joke he played on me. Yeah, we were funny that way. Flatts had taken over The Saloon, from my grandfather. Nothing hostile, Pop was just looking to unload one of the bars.

Flatts was a staunch Irishman, from County Meath. He was the real deal right down to the accent. My grandfather helped him come to the United States as a favor for the DeEsso cartel. He had been very good at transporting goods and was called upon for various needs. As fate would have it, he got pinched for smuggling from Northern Ireland and had to flee the country. He wasn't completely into the darker parts of this thing we do. In fact, when he handled a weapon, he always held it like it was on fire or something. So I would always be careful with what I involved him in, but he was an asset nevertheless.

So anyway, I entered the basement and I kid you not, there was Dante hanging from a pipe, his pants were around his ankles and his junk was hanging out.

"I thought you were going to shoot him?" I asked Benny.

"Not yet, first I have to make a few adjustments to his mechanics," Benny replied, followed by a sinister half of a laugh.

So what does Benny do? He had that infamous wrench out, which was the size of an arm. He was whacking Dante in the nuts over and over again. I now knew why I'd heard those girly shrieks from upstairs. He hit him so many times I felt it myself and almost started feeling bad for the guy. Benny never said much, but I noticed when he hit the guy, he had a word for every whack. I looked at him, puzzled.

"What the fuck are you doing?"

Benny turned toward me, raising the wrench and waving it like an orchestra conductor, "It's a syllable beating. I learned it from my father. One whack for every syllable. It's very rewarding."

I just looked at him and said to the Hamburglar, "You're lucky he's not reading the Gettysburg Address." In reality, I was thinking to myself that the guy probably would have preferred a quick shot to the head.

"Benny, just end it. He's pretty much unconscious anyway."

"Absolutely," Benny said. "But what lesson have we learned? Everybody's got to follow the fucking rules. You're either weak or you're strong. I prefer strong."

I replied, "But I call the shots, so, end it now."

Benny pulled out his gun, pointed it at Dante's head and after pulling the trigger, skull fragments went flying everywhere. He didn't stop there, though. Then he pointed the gun at the guy's junk and shot that too, blowing it right off.

"You needed to do that?" I asked, amazed at how thorough Benny was.

"Yeah, for effect," said Benny. "If you're gonna do a job, you may as well do it right."

Benny and I were sorting through the next steps when we heard some noise from the top of the stairs. I turned around and well, you're not going to believe this, but who comes walking down the steps while Dante's hanging there, bleeding like a pig? Samantha, that's who. I guess I forgot to lock the door and she let herself in. I really have to stop drinking.

One look at Dante and she started screaming at the top of her lungs, calling me every name you can think of and she started running towards Benny in anger. Imagine that, Dante is dead and she's complaining to the guy who killed him. Well, she was number two on the list, so I figured, what the hell.

"Go for it, Benny." I waved my hand in disgust. I couldn't believe this was happening. It was one of those moments in life when you think 'damn, just when I thought I saw everything.'

Benny grabbed her and she looked at me. Sam looked scared, but defiant as well. I don't think Samantha understood the gravity of the situation. The fact that she was caught with this guy's dick inside of her didn't resonate enough and was she stupid enough to think that I didn't know about the other guys? I've got eyes and ears all over town, stupid bitch. So, she turned towards me and asked, "You're gonna kill me too, Thomas?"

I smiled a little, pleased with my newest recruit and happy to give him some more work, "No, I wouldn't do that, darling, but he is," pointing at Benny.

Samantha was still running her mouth, talking about how she never loved me and would have fucked my brothers if she'd had the chance. Benny had had enough and whacked her right in the mouth with that wrench. It sounded like glass broke when it hit her teeth. I said, "Just shoot her and get it over with."

THE BEGINNING

Samantha was still coherent and somehow that mouth was still running. She was on her knees at this point. She started acting desperate, pleading with Benny and me to show some mercy. "I'm sorry, Tommy, I really am. I just wanted some attention and you were never around. I love you, we're supposed to get married..." What happened next proved why Benny is so feared and revered. I kid you not, he picked up Dante's dick, shoved it in her mouth and said, "This should taste familiar." Samantha's eyes bulged out of her face. I guess the familiar taste couldn't calm her. It was just as well as I couldn't really understand what she was saying with half her teeth hanging out of her mouth and the rest on the floor.

I just stared at Benny in awe and said, "Let me guess, for effect, right?"

Benny looked at me, chuckled and threw a sideways smirk towards Samantha, who looked like she was still trying to talk. Benny then blew half her face clean off. The girl didn't stand a chance.

Just in case you weren't following that, I had a bloodbath in the basement. Benny was unfamiliar with our disposal policy, so I gave him the phone number of Mr. Dwyer, who ran the local crematorium. He was a dear friend of my Grandfather's and owed us many favors.

"Give him a call and a total. Tell him it's for a barbeque. Dwyer will take care of the rest," I told Benny.

And just like that, I had to find a new date for tonight. And a new line cook.

54

CHAPTER TEN

Frank:

All of a sudden, my cousin Tommy wasn't engaged anymore. Samantha had disappeared and was nowhere to be found. The whole family was looking for her. They posted pictures on every telephone pole on the street, like she was a lost dog.

I walked into the bar to see my cousin. Everything was like a landmark with Tommy. You always knew when he'd done something to elevate him to another level because he created an effect that screamed, 'look at me and what I have just done.' Today was no exception. He sat at the bar, a light shining directly overhead so it could illuminate his face to look like it was glowing, almost like a fucking angel. But Tommy was no angel and the glow was more like the devil, with the embers of evil surrounding him.

I just stared at him. And then, there was that infamous smirk. Every time my cousin did something he wasn't supposed to, his face gave him away, but only I knew it. It scared the shit out of me. I always wondered what I would do if he looked at me that way too. Despite it all,

Samantha was missing and I had to ask, even if I already had an inkling of what the answer was.

"Cousin, what happened with Samantha? I heard you guys had a falling out," I asked.

"Yeah, we had an argument. She took off Frank and I haven't seen her since. You know Samantha, here one day, gone the next. Well, this was one of those fights where I think she may never be found."

I let Tommy's story sink in and took it for the truth. What was I going to do? I had no reason not to believe him. However, he didn't seem too shaken up or concerned about her disappearance.

*　　　*　　　*

Anthony:

Tommy's engagement didn't last and Frank got Mary pregnant, so I guess that made me the smartest one of the three. I was just dating around. There was this one girl in particular that I liked, but I never did well with long-term relationships. Let's just say I wasn't always a perfect gentleman.

"Anthony, every time we go out, you barely say, two words," my latest girl, Barbara, said as she took a long sip of her wine, glaring at me over the glass.

Barbara had a dynamite body, but those eyes could cut through you like hot steel through butter. "Really, Barbara? You want me to use two words? I've got two words for you... Hand. Job."

"What?" she asked, flabbergasted.

"Yeah, hand-job. As in, I could use one."

She looked at me and said, "Is that how you ask? What's going on with you, Anthony? Hair slicked back, fancy leather jacket on? You think you're some kind of big shot now?" Between those looks she gave and that sharp mouth of hers, I'd had enough. I got up from the table, thought about grabbing her by her hair and forcing her into the car. I thought about pulling that skirt up to her waist and having my way with her, but that bitch, she didn't even deserve that. I took a few dollars out of my pocket, threw it on the table and walked out. Fuck her!

*   *   *

Frank:

I very rarely drank, but knowing that Mary was pregnant and her parents didn't know, I needed an outlet to vent my frustration about not being able to support her financially. I went to The Saloon. The bar was empty, but as I sat down, I heard a familiar voice come up from behind me.

"Hey, Frank?" I rolled my eyes, because I knew who it was, although she was the last person I was expecting to show up in this bar. I turned around and sure as shit, it was Paige Brown. I hadn't seen her in years. She used to hang around with my friends and me at the bars. She came from money and we could never figure out what she was doing with us. It sometimes felt like she lived on the other side of the world. She was pretty, but she was fucking annoying, too. "Hi, Frank, how've ya been?"

I took a long look at her, trying to figure out how much to offer up. What was on her mind? Why was she here and alone? Was she looking for me? I dismissed those thoughts and finally responded, "Pretty good, what've you been up to? It's been a while."

"I finished college and got a job with the local paper," she said proudly.

Not many from our time finished college, or even went for that matter, so she had a right to boast. Although, in true Paige style, she was a little too proud.

"No shit, you're a writer now?" I fed her ego a little just to see where it was going.

"Not just any writer, an investigative reporter."

Oh. Shit. Here we go. "Wow, didn't see that coming," I lied. We all knew Paige was that kind, always nagging and annoying and now it seemed that she had an angle as well. I started to think that this was not a chance meeting after all.

"So, how's your crazy cousin, Tommy?" Paige asked.

"He's fine. You haven't gone over to Ron's recently?" I replied as the red flags went up in my mind. 'Careful here, Frank,' I told myself, reinforcing the need to stick to the script.

"No, I just moved out of my parent's house and I'm setting myself up about a mile from here. How's Mary?" she asked hesitantly. "I'm, uh, hearing things, Frank."

"Like?" And now I'm really thinking, here we go. That was what always drove me nuts about Paige. She was always asking people personal shit. She was a nosy fuck. "Okay, I'll bite. What did you hear, Paige?" I sighed and took a big gulp of my drink.

"I heard you're gonna be a Dad." Shit, nobody ever put it like that. Most people said, "You and Mary are expecting?" Or, "She's pregnant?" Paige's blunt and honest statement hit me like a ton of bricks. Sometimes things don't seem real until they are presented in a way that resonates with you and Paige succeeded with that.

I tried not to seem too shaken up. "Well, it looks that way," I said, hoping that it would end the conversation and she would go away.

"Okay, well, congratulations, can I buy you a drink?" Reluctantly, I said yes. Lately, I've been drinking a bit more than usual. I never turn down free booze. It was amazing that something so meaningful could be watered down with the clink of a couple of ice cubes in a glass and a long swig of Tito's.

THE BEGINNING

So, Paige and I had a few. She looked good, but even better when she shut the fuck up. And when I wasn't getting the third-degree, it was nice to bullshit with someone who didn't have a vested interest in my day-to-day activities. But, I knew Mary wasn't far behind, she was always tracking me. As the night went on, things got a little weird and I thought maybe Paige and I would leave together. It was a little too comfortable for me, but it was all interrupted by a tap on my shoulder. Sure as hell, it was Mary.

"Paige! Got nothing fuckin' else to do?" Mary said, in a way only an Italian woman could say it. With her hands on her hips and her eyes looking around the room for whatever she could use to whack Paige. Mary was short and unassuming, but that never stopped her from being larger than life when she was angered.

"Oh, hey, Mary," Paige said, almost falling off the barstool because she was either drunk or in shock. "I'm just hanging out with my friend, Frankie here." Paige slurred and put her hands on my shoulder to steady herself, as she got up. I thought Mary was going to blow, but before she could, Paige slipped off to the bathroom.

"Get your shit and let's get out of here, Frank," Mary demanded, angry as all hell. I didn't have a choice in the matter, so I slid off the bar stool, stole one last glance at the bathroom door and staggered home with Mary.

ALLIANCE

A few days later, I went over to Ron's to see Tommy, for our monthly poker night. I walked in and there were some unfamiliar faces there. Tommy ushered me over and said, "I want you to meet a few of my associates. Benny, this is my cousin, Frankie and this is Scopa."

"Nice to meet you guys. Can I get a word, Tommy?" We went off to the side of the bar, but I noticed how Benny eyeballed me the whole time.

"Is that Benny Costa?" I asked, knowing full well what the answer was, but needing Tommy to explain what he was doing here.

"Uh, yeah. How'd you know?" Tommy asked.

"Did you forget that we share the same Grandfather?" I snarled at him.

Tommy replied, with a chuckle, "From time to time."

Glaring at him, I responded, "I don't think it's funny. Of all people, Benny is a serious kind of person to have on your team. What? You're not handling things yourself anymore? All of a sudden, you need help? This is not like you Tommy. You usually know everything about everything and never needed any outside help."

"Never mind that, what's this shit about you joining the police department?"

"It's not shit, it's a certainty. I've been hired. Anthony, too."

THE BEGINNING

Tommy took a deep breath and let out a puff of smoke from his cigarette. "How did you manage to pull that off? Didn't any questions come up about me during your background check? They're supposed to know about these things and they missed your connection to Grandpa and me? I guess we're flying under the radar, just like we should."

"No. I've managed to keep it on the hush-hush. Nobody is asking and nobody will."

"Okay, so let me think. This doesn't have to be a bad thing," Tommy said, stroking his chin.

I saw his wheels turning and that mind of his was thinking about how he could turn this into an opportunity to advance his business.

"I can run any trucks up and down the road now, with anything I see fit to put in them," Tommy murmured, "And…"

"Stop right there," I interrupted. "Cousin, there's no way I'm getting involved in anything, with you that's illegal, so don't fucking ask. I haven't even pinned a badge on yet and you already have me going to jail."

"Whoa, easy Frankie. Now you have big balls all of a sudden and are going to tell me what to do, or not to do?"

"Balls nothing. Nobody really gives a shit about us being related and I want to keep it that way. It has nothing to do with me and you. I'm not

62

in your business now and me being a cop has nothing to do with us. Let's keep it that way. You and Grandpa ought to get that straight right out of the gate."

"Whatever you say, cousin. I'm proud of you. Is that what you want me to say? From the looks of it, it doesn't seem like you even give a shit about us being related," Tommy added, storming off.

I stood there and watched him walk towards the new guys. I looked at Scopa and wondered, "Who's this guy?" I didn't know about Scopa and that was even scarier than knowing who Benny was. At least with Benny, you knew what you were going to get. You knew who he was and what he was here to do. This Scopa guy was an unknown and I just had to hope that I didn't get caught up in the middle of all these new faces.

*   *   *

Anthony:

Frank met me at the gym, where we were supposed to get in another good workout. We were getting ready to join the police department and were using the gym to get in shape. We knew there were going to be times we would need not only our strength, but our ability to fight, in order to settle things down in those rough neighborhoods. Hell, our neighborhood was one of the worst and we did all right there.

Frank didn't seem like himself. He was not into working out and clearly there was something troubling him.

"Let me ask you something Anthony, who's this guy Scopa?"

"You mean, I know something about your cousin before you do?"

That conversation could have gone one of two ways. Either Frank could ask too many questions, or make too many assumptions about Tommy and his associates. Either way, I needed to do one thing, which was, to keep myself out of it.

"Cut the shit Anthony, who is he?"

"If you must know, Frank, he was one of the top hundred poker players in the United States, hence the name, Scopa. He's a business associate of Tommy's and I think I really shouldn't be talking to you about this. Why don't you ask your cousin yourself?"

I wasn't gonna tell Frank who this guy was, but he really should have asked Tommy himself. We were both getting into the police department. Quite frankly, I shouldn't have known who Scopa was either, but sticking close to Tommy, you couldn't help but notice the kind of company he was keeping.

Tommy's crew was growing and getting stronger with the addition of Benny and Scopa. As the story goes, Scopa had an issue while he was playing cards, let's say a "legal matter" that forced him to disappear from the spotlight. In addition to being a great card player, he had a stake in many business deals on the East Coast. Tommy brought him in as a finance monitor. His job was collections. He had a heavy hand and used it to make sure Tommy's customers paid their bills.

Tommy was already dealing with Flatts on business projects in Florida and New Jersey and made Scopa the liaison between the two. I never told Frank this, but I started to go on some of the collections with Tommy from time to time. I needed some extra cash while we were waiting to get in the police department and that was an easy way to pick up a few extra bucks as added security.

Although Scopa was the big man and he threw his weight around to get the results he needed, his methods were much different than Benny's. But Tommy knew what he was doing. He was assembling an army.

*   *   *

Tommy:

I knew Frank was a little concerned when he saw Benny and I understood why. This was a family business. We never really went outside of our own, mostly because you could never trust anyone who was not connected. Family meant just that, family. When Benny came into the picture, I knew I had to make him part of my crew. Who knows, maybe I'm a genius or maybe it's one of the biggest mistakes I'll ever make.

I was a little different. Grandpa always kept it in-house, but he also never expanded beyond what his capabilities allowed him to. I was looking to grow, to branch out beyond New York and Florida. I even hired a front-man for all my property and the legal part of my finances. Like all good gangsters, I was looking to hold onto as much money as I could. Part of that meant that I had to find ways to funnel cash to some kind of legitimate enterprise.

Enter Joe Knapp, who was a straight-up kind of guy. He was the son of one of Grandpa's close associates. They kept him out of the family business, but he was a financial whiz and I needed him to make my businesses seem legit. He was the perfect front man. Plus, he could be trusted, because he grew up around this life, around Grandpa and me. Like I said before, family is family, and Joe, well, he was like family.

We met one afternoon to go over business. I had to give him some direction on a new venture and I wanted to make sure he understood what I expected. I was not into throwing good money after bad and expected that my project would bring a profit if you know what I mean.

"Joe, I'm opening up a new bar in Florida. I want you to get down there, make sure it goes smooth and keep my name out of it."

"No problem, Tommy, same as the last one? Just make sure there's a money train coming back to New York, correct?" Joe asked.

"That's what I like about you, Joe: straight and to the point. You get where I am at, right away. No lying in you. I like that."

"The last thing I want to do is lie. People like that don't last too long around here," Joe hesitantly laughed.

"That's an understatement, Joe. People that lie die a slow, painful death."

You could see Joe was nervous. He grabbed his glass of wine, raised it and said, "To success" and tipped his glass. He almost gulped the whole thing down in one shot.

Guys like Joe were the best to have around. Obviously, they were not there for the more physical part of the job but, hey, you needed a Brady Bunch kind of look to at least appear as if you were legit. Joe fit that part perfectly and more importantly, he was too scared to want to fuck up.

CHAPTER ELEVEN

Frank:

Today was the first day at the Police Academy for Anthony and me. It was like going to boot camp and I say that without knowing what boot camp is really like because I was never in the military. It was quasi-military, with the instructors thinking they were teaching a bunch of recruits who were going to war. It was just a different kind of war, that's all. So, it was not a stretch to say I wasn't surprised when the first thing they did was look us up and down, from the length of our hair to how shiny our shoes were.

Growing up in the area that we did, it was really difficult to take any kind of direction from anyone, let alone police officers who were like drill instructors for sixteen weeks. One of the adjunct instructors was an FBI agent. His name was Agent Robert Carter and you didn't have to talk to him long to know two things: he was as straight as an arrow and as smart as a whip.

"Anthony," I whispered, as we sat in the back of the classroom, "Who is this guy? He's looking at me like he's known me for a thousand years."

"He's an FBI agent, Frank. Maybe it's one of his tactics, he's probably just trying to throw you off," Anthony said, as he shrugged his shoulders.

I tried to believe Anthony and thought maybe my mind was playing tricks on me. But the more I thought about it, the more I figured out what was going on. This guy probably knew my family and that scared the living shit out of me.

*   *   *

Anthony:

Doing anything with Frank used to drive me crazy, let alone attending the Police Academy with him. I came prepared that day because I wanted to shine. I needed to get as far away from where I had been and this seemed like my ticket out. I wanted to distance myself as much as possible from the street. I needed to be anyone but Anthony Crespo, from Willard Street.

Frank was right about Robert Carter. He didn't have to say much for me to know he knew who we were. I don't like to use big words, but our lives were polarized by Frank and Tommy's Grandfather and the legacy Tommy was trying to carve out. This guy Carter was no dummy and why he didn't single us out right away was a mystery to me. I was fully expecting that we would be called in and told our services were no longer needed. Maybe there was another plan. Whatever was going on,

I was going to keep my eyes open, my ears to the ground and my mouth shut.

Frank was unprepared that day. He didn't do his homework. I don't know if Frank was playing stupid, or did not understand the fact that the Academy was serious business. He was not going to be able to skate by on his good looks alone. The instructors were none too pleased with him and went up one side of him and down the other, but to Frank's credit, he took it. He did not mouth off, which shocked me in a way. Frank could be proud, too proud sometimes, to the point where he could hurt himself. But this time around, he showed me something and I was surprised. Maybe Frank really wanted to play it straight, maybe he really wanted to be a cop.

The other observation I made about Frank sent a chill down my spine. It was when I noticed Carter talking to him, just conversing really, but a little too casually for an instructor to be talking to a recruit. It was very unusual since all the other instructors were like drill sergeants and treated the recruits like maggots. There simply was no casual conversation at all.

*   *   *

Frank:

"Robert Carter," he said, as he offered his hand to me.

"Yes, Sir, Frank Risi, nice to meet you." I grabbed his hand in a tight grip.

Carter stared at me for a second. It was like he was studying me, taking me in. Maybe he was sizing me up in an effort to determine what I was doing there. To tell you the truth, the whole thing was a bit awkward. Carter had been part of our orientation and made it clear we would not speak unless spoken to. Everything was 'Sir' and very regimented. For him to be speaking to me so casually was strange. Carter was about ten years older than me and was a highly decorated Agent assigned to a field office in our area. There was no doubt about how good he was, otherwise, he would not be at the Academy training recruits. Plus, all you had to do was look at this guy and you knew he meant business.

"Risi, is it? Hmmm, what had you been doing Cadet Risi, prior to the Academy?"

I was taken aback again, and almost immediately I was thinking, here it comes. This guy knows the family, knows what Tommy is doing. Just what do I tell this guy that will fly? I looked at him and managed a confident reply, "I was a builder, working for private companies." It was the truth and I had nothing to hide, but I also didn't want to find myself in a position where I had to defend my family.

"Really?" He seemed surprised but was still not letting on to what his special interest was in me.

I started scratching my head. It was like he was looking at me as if he'd just won a lottery but didn't want to seem too excited. Anyway, it was time for physical training and thank God, too. The funny thing was, he never stopped looking me in the eye and even stranger was that he never let go of my hand. It was like he was using the handshake as some sort of lie detector test. It was very creepy.

"Excuse me, Sir?" The drill instructor interrupted, breaking the awkward feeling I was experiencing.

"Um, yeah," Carter said, not letting go of my hand, and still staring at me.

"Sir, this Cadet needs to get to the gym for PT."

Carter snapped out of it and replied, "Oh yes," and let go of my hand.

"May I be excused?" I asked.

"Certainly, by all means." I started walking away, but not quickly enough. "Oh, Cadet?"

I turned back towards Carter, waiting for his response. He replied quickly, "It was really nice meeting you."

"Yes. Nice meeting you, too."

Carter replied, "Nice meeting me, too?" with the sternness I was expecting earlier.

"I meant, Sir."

"Well then say it, Cadet," he barked.

"Nice meeting you, Sir!"

As I walked away, I was thinking, what a prick.

Anthony came close to me, "What did he want?"

"I'm not sure," I replied. "Anyway, let's go. I need this fucking job and don't want to jeopardize it by kicking his ass."

The whole encounter with Carter made me think. What was I up against with this job? Would my reputation precede me? Wait... I had a reputation? I'd like to think I was so distant from Grandpa and Tommy and their business dealings that I could pave my own road. I think maybe my first mistake was believing that I could escape that world. My second was to be so naive as to think all Carter wanted to do was feel me out to see if I was legit or not. No matter, I was going to play this straight and what happened next was out of my hands.

*   *   *

Anthony:

"So, you gonna tell me what Carter wanted, or what?" I asked Frank, prying a little bit more.

"Nothing really and why are you so interested all of a sudden? Do you think I'm going to tell him all about Tommy, or Grandpa, for that matter?"

"I am interested because it seems like a lot more than just nothing. The look on his face... man, it looked like he'd struck gold. I know what you said, that you didn't tell him anything. C'mon did he ask about me, or Tommy, or about the family? You know that Carter knows who we are, he has to be looking to find out why we're here. Do you really think that Carter believes we just want to be cops?"

"Anthony, please. Shut – the – fuck – up."

I could tell I was pushing Frank's buttons, but I needed to know what was going on. My end goal was to join the FBI and this Carter guy might be my ticket in. I knew I could use his interest in Frank to my advantage. If I could position myself to where what I knew about the streets got me into the bureau, so be it. But I wasn't a rat. I had to be careful not to let Frank know my real intentions because with the connections we had, being a cop is one thing, being an FBI agent was completely another.

"All right, Frankie, calm down. Save your energy for PT. I didn't mean anything by it, I was just curious. That's all."

The PT drills were grueling and a couple of the cadets even lost their lunch. Frank and I did all right and somehow we managed to be among the first to finish up the drills. We were running back to the locker

74

rooms to get changed for an evening class when Frank asked me, "Do you think that agent knows who my family is?"

I probably shouldn't have egged him on earlier, since it might have planted a seed in his mind or something and I knew better than to be straight with Frank because the truth might have forced him to drop out of the Academy. "Nah, Frank, you just have one of those faces. Like you're familiar or something," I said, as I punched him on the arm.

Frank stopped for a second to think about that and his face told me he decided to believe me. That was probably one of the only times in my life I was happy I wasn't related to those two fucks.

CHAPTER TWELVE

Frank:

"Babe, listen, these shifts are killing me, too, but what am I supposed to do? I haven't been in this job long enough to pick my own hours. There's no way I'm not going to work the overnights."

I pleaded with Mary. She was upset. I wasn't home as much as she wanted and I tried to make her understand the need to be patient. With a kid, a house to take care of and a meager budget, it was a struggle for all of us.

"I know Frank, but can't you just ask? I mean, you're gone all night and you sleep all day. What about us?" Mary asked as she motioned towards Frank Jr.

I wasn't prepared for this, or so I thought. I still felt like a kid myself but thought I was doing the right thing by joining the force. The assignment I had was a tough one and the department was fourth highest in workload in New York State. Crack was rampant and I was assigned to a walking post in the worst part of the city. We had twenty-one homicides in a two-square-mile area that year. They were killing each other over drug territory and I was right in the middle of it all.

76

ALLIANCE

In those days, the late 1980's, we were involved in a lot of hand-to-hand combat. Don't get me wrong, we had shootings, but most issues were settled on the streets with our fists. What made our jobs more difficult was that Anthony and I knew many of the people we were dealing with, in one way or another. Since we were in the same squad, Anthony and I relied on each other for survival. We had to deal with gangs and organized crime. Believe it or not, there were also many celebrities you would never believe were addicts. They visited our side of town regularly. That was until they were read about in the paper and ended up being sent to a rehab.

"Listen, Mary, I get it, and I'm sorry. Until I can make rank, this is the only schedule I can work."

I gave her a hug and kissed her. She kissed me back and in a way that I knew what she wanted. My mind and body were so tired, but I gave in to her, picked her up and carried her into the bedroom. I threw her on the bed and gave it to her good and a little rough, just like she liked it. Mary was great in bed, but I was still worried that she wasn't getting enough from me as a husband. She was feeding those doubts more frequently. When you are young and have a family, you think working is enough. There was so much more people needed to feel relevant.

After we were done in the bedroom, Mary told me that she had run into Tommy earlier that day.

"Yeah, I haven't seen much of him, what, with being busy with shift work," I told her.

"Well, he asked about you. Tommy wanted to know when you were working and where you were assigned. He even asked who your commanding officer was and if you had a partner. It was a lot of questions."

"Really?" I didn't say much more, but I knew what Tommy was doing. What may have seemed like genuine interest was him scoping out the territory. He was trying to figure out what he was up against, or who he had on his side. Basically, what was in it for the family? It was same old Tommy, always looking out for his own self-interest, and I knew that he did not care who he hurt in the process.

CHAPTER THIRTEEN

Frank:

It had been several years now since Anthony and I joined the police department. While you're on the job, you evolve and end up leaning towards a particular niche. Some loved the road and going from job to job, some just liked being traffic cops and then there were promotions to specialized units. We had already won one of the highest awards in the county. We took first prize for bravery. The job was starting to take over our lives, though. You see, it was never just a job, it was a lifestyle. That's what a lot of people could never understand. For Anthony, he saw it as simply a step towards being a Fed. For me, it was something I had no idea I would ever be doing.

The violence and the fighting were just part of those times. No matter what type of call you went on, none was more unpredictable than a domestic.

One night Anthony and I were doing patrol and responded to a husband and wife dispute. The neighbors called after they heard yelling and were worried.

"Mr. Jones, your wife made a complaint. I'm sorry, but you're going to have to leave for the night." I spoke calmly and cautiously.

Mr. Jones was a big man and procedure was open to interpretation, which included having to lock up this crazy son of a bitch if he was not going to go quietly.

I looked at Anthony, and whispered, "He's not going to leave."

"Be quiet," Anthony replied.

"Now, Mr. Jones, you can come back tomorrow, please gather your things," I said.

Picture this, we were in this guy's house and his wife was at the dinner table, running her mouth. Anthony and I were trying to plead with a guy twice our size and asking him to calmly leave. Well, he wasn't calm and about twenty feet behind us was the front door with a wooden frame and multiple window panes.

Mr. Jones, replied, booming, "You boys need to go. I'm not leaving my house. This bitch can go, but I pay the rent, the light, the cable, and for all the other shit in this place, so I ain't leaving."

Anthony replied, "Fuck."

I continued to work my magic, or at least try to. "Mr. Jones, your wife made you dinner laced with Ajax. That's an indication you need to take a break, right?"

ALLIANCE

I don't know how he didn't see the blue powder underneath the chicken. Did he think it was cayenne pepper?

"I told you guys to leave," he said and then he grabbed me and Anthony and drove us through the closed door. Of course, it was closed. Closed, locked and very solid. We crashed through it so fast we didn't even feel it. I then found myself on the sidewalk, glass and wood all over me.

I started yelling to Anthony, "Grab something, anything," as I shouted into the radio, "13 to headquarters. 10-13, officer needs assistance."

Those were the only words I could get out before the situation turned into a full-fledged melee. It was a "battle-royale" and I was not ready to be the loser in that mess, especially since this guy was no longer mad at his wife. Instead, he was full-on furious with us.

I managed to grab my handcuffs and apply one to Mr. Jones' wrist. I knew we were in real trouble since once I got a handcuff on him, it only closed on to the first click. The guy had massive wrists and it was not because he was fat.

Needless to say, our street-side came out in Anthony and me, as we hit that guy with everything but the kitchen sink. Finally, Anthony got a cuff on the other hand and we were able to link them together. What a fucking night. But that's how it was at any given moment and I was beginning to think that maybe I would be safer working for Tommy. Then again, maybe not, because in Tommy's work, you weren't brawling, you were just dead.

THE BEGINNING

*   *   *

Anthony:

Frank was different to me now. We were protecting one another, watching each other's back, so it was hard not to bond. Frank was usually good at talking to people, save the Mr. Jones' of the world. I could see he was on the path leading to the Detective Division. Frank was a rising star and there was no mistake about that.

Most people think you need to be a Rhodes Scholar to make rank. It's true, you need to be able to answer reading comprehension questions to make sergeant and higher on the civil service test. But, if you were going to be a Detective, you needed real talent that went beyond just the book.

Most good detectives will tell you the gift of the gab is the ticket to success. Think about it, you need to be able to have a casual conversation with some low life scumbag who just stabbed his mother to death, with the aim of getting him to confess, in writing, without the benefit of some greasy lawyer fucking it up for you. That takes real talent.

The thing about that was, of all people, Frank had a real knack for doing just that. He could get a blind man to confess that he stole a pair of glasses because he needed them to read the newspaper that day. And he could then get the guy to swear to it all in court, including the fact that he didn't want a lawyer. Frank was just that good.

CHAPTER
FOURTEEN

Frank:

A couple of fellow officers, Rosa and Jameson, and I were starting to do a lot of work with Terry Robinson, a detective assigned to the street crime unit in a neighboring jurisdiction. Along with the work came a lot of partying. That was not sitting well with Mary, who was losing her patience with me even before Terry came into the picture.

There were three bars on one strip, The Saloon, Ron's, and The Fox Hole. Ron's and the Fox Hole were owned by Tommy. The Saloon was across the street and it was incredible, with a lot of natural beauty. It had a huge painting of the American Flag on one wall that stretched as high as the upstairs loft. Tommy was there so much, you would think he owned it, too. The Saloon and The Fox Hole had exotic dancers, which didn't sit favorably with the wives. But it made for an interesting place to drink. Plus, with Tommy around, I never had to pay for any drinks and who could argue with that. Pretty ladies with next to nothing on and free drinks, it was the perfect combination. It could almost make a guy forget that he was married.

THE BEGINNING

Anyway, one night we were all in The Saloon. My cousin was having one of his regular card nights and all the usual suspects were parked in their familiar places at the bar. I walked in with Terry and Anthony, who, by the way, couldn't stand each other. Two people, in the same field, going in two different directions was not a good mix. And for Terry and Anthony, they could not be more different.

Terry was flashy. Some would say he even modeled himself after the movie hero, Shaft, who was the lord of the streets and master of his own destiny. Everyone knows that cops have egos, but Terry was in another galaxy when it came to being overconfident. Anthony could not be more different. He was a gritty cop, who was mired in the dirt of the street. He worked narcotics and this is where he and Terry crossed paths. They would use each other's CI's (confidential informants) from time to time, when they weren't bickering with each other. In the police business, sharing anything, especially CI's was not kosher.

*   *   *

Anthony:

I hated that fucking guy Robinson, flashy cocksucker. My relationship with Agent Carter was growing and I was taking the steps necessary to become an FBI agent and move on.

When we went to bars, I did all I could to avoid Terry. It was bad enough that he was stealing my sources to make himself look good, but he had to hang with me and Frank, too. He was not from the neighborhood, he wasn't even Italian, so why would he want to hang in a bar of neighborhood guys, where he clearly did not belong? I didn't get it, but then again, like I said, I hated that cocksucker.

"Where's Tommy?" I asked Frank.

Frank replied, "I heard he is in the loft with Flatts. You know, Tommy. He's into proving his manhood lately. I wouldn't be surprised if they have a couple of girls up there. Let's sneak up there and see what's going on."

Terry went to the bar to get a drink while Anthony and I headed up to the loft. What did we see when we got up there? Tommy was getting a blow job on one side of the room and Flatts was getting one on the other. Fuckers were using a stopwatch to see who could hold out the longest. It was the most ludicrous, yet funniest thing I had seen in a while.

I shook my head and said, "Look at these idiots." Frank grabbed a long pretzel stick and started touching Tommy's back. Flatts couldn't see us. It preoccupied Tommy just long enough and then we heard it. Flatts yelled out, as he let go in the girl's mouth. It was funny, because Flatts, in his thick Irish accent, yelled, "For fuck's sake, here it comes."

We stood up and Frankie waved to Flatts, with the pretzel stick. Flatts shot back, "You son of a bitch you cheated," as he slammed a couple of hundreds on the table. The two girls ran downstairs, the one that was with Flatts was covering her mouth. Yeah, it was crude and dirty, but that was what Tommy had become. And being from the streets, that mentality came out in us despite all the work we put in to try and become civil. It is amazing how quickly you can regress back to being a heathen.

"Hello girls," I laughed, as they ran past us and I couldn't resist messing with the one girl covering her mouth. "What's the matter, your mouth glued shut?" Everyone was laughing, spitting out their drinks. It reminded me of when we were kids and would do all kinds of crazy shit together. It was almost as if nothing had changed between us, but in reality, lots had changed because Frank and I weren't the ones getting blowjobs from strange girls. In fact, we were locking guys up who were paying for girls like those.

I went downstairs to the bar, which was filling up with people. Jameson was there, talking to Paige Brown and Terry.

"How have you been?" I asked Paige.

"Very good and even better now, that one of these fine gentlemen bought me a drink," Paige said, lifting her glass and grinning.

"Let me guess, Jameson paid, right?"

Paige replied, "How did you know?"

"I knew because Terry over here is too cheap to buy anyone anything," I answered, motioning to Robinson. Everyone chuckled at my joke, except Terry.

"Easy there, fella," Terry cut in. "I'm economically conservative, never cheap, just frugal."

Paige turned to Frank and in unison, they parroted, "He's a cheap bastard."

*   *   *

Frank:

When I wasn't working with Anthony, I was with Jameson. He had been on the job a little longer than me and was better than halfway done with his career. He had plans to retire when he hit twenty years and move to the Virgin Islands. Jameson had this idea that he was going to spend the rest of his days enjoying the good life. He would captain a fishing boat during the day and then stay drunk all night. What a life, just not very realistic for an accomplished guy like him.

Jameson was smart and he was about to be made detective. He had a way with women, but unlike Terry, he was a lot less conspicuous about it. Jameson was bold and brash and made no effort to hide what he was thinking, which most of the time was figuring out how to get laid.

He was seeing Paige on and off. Through him, Paige made it her business to know all of us better. Newspaper people sometimes do that to get closer to the source. It wasn't that Paige was a whore or anything, we all kind of knew what she was up to, even Jameson. There was no mystery as to what was going on.

The other thing that was going on with Paige was that she stood out from the crowd. Mostly because she and Jameson were an interracial relationship and she did nothing to hide it. In fact, she sometimes bragged about it in a strange way. I remember her coming out of the bathroom at the bar with him, with a look of pride on her face. Believe it or not, I think she actually liked him as a person and not just as a source of information.

One day she was drinking and in a dead stare, she pointed at Jameson and tipped her drink saying, "I'm not the first white woman and I won't be the last." That was Paige, just when you figured her out she would go and say some shit that would stop a person in their tracks.

What do you expect? When you hang out in a bar all the time, all kinds of drama happens.

My work with Terry was becoming more complex and the bar usually provided the perfect outlet for us to talk about strategy. The biggest problem was keeping Anthony and him from fighting, especially since now we were all working on a drug investigation together. It involved a newly organized crime group on 48th Street. It was so bad, even Tommy noticed the shake-up. The new trafficking team was affecting both mine and Terry's jurisdiction. More importantly, it was impacting Tommy's pocket, and the last thing we needed were bodies dropping.

CHAPTER FIFTEEN

Frank:

I had sort of expected that this was going to happen. I had been sent for. Yes, it was just like in those mafia movies, where you know you are going to get whacked but you go anyway. It was Tommy who was calling and I knew exactly why.

"Frank, what's all this shit about a drug war on my turf?" Tommy asked, even before I was through the front door of his house. "Not only do you fucking cops have these guys dealing right in front of my businesses, but you're letting these half-assed jamokes move in on my neighborhood?" Tommy was in my face, I could feel his breath as he yelled at me. I stood strong next to him, trying to maintain my cool. I knew he was mad and was taking it out on me. But, I wasn't going to let my guard down.

"Your neighborhood?" I hissed back. I looked at Tommy as though he was half crazy. "Tommy, you have to understand that I'm not part of your crew. It's not my job to look out for your interests. It's my job to be a cop. Maybe you forgot that!"

"What you forgot, cousin, is that you are family and that will never change. So whatever you and your flunky drug squad have to do to calm things down, it better get done. Or, I will do it myself and then your little community will know what real violence is about. *Capisce?*"

Deep inside I knew that Tommy was right, not about the family, but about us. The police needed to restore order in the neighborhood and that was going to fall on me, Anthony, and Terry and there was no getting away from it. We could not become Tommy's pawns in the process, though.

So I just looked at Tommy, nodded and replied, *"Capisce,* cousin," letting him think that he had gotten to me and that I was in his pocket. Regardless of everything else, I still had to be careful with Tommy, because he could be ruthless, even with family.

*   *   *

Tommy:

The shit about Samantha finally died down and business was good, thanks to that sit-down I had with Frank. Every once in a while you have to smack a guy in the mouth to get him to see reason. With Frank, that smack came when you talked about family. See, while Frank acted all tough, he had a weak spot and it was me, Grandpa, and believe it or not, Anthony, too. I just needed to exploit it a little. Now if I could get my own life in order, all would be right in the world once more.

THE BEGINNING

As usual, all the problems I had centered around the family. What else was there? As it was, I wasn't talking to my father, which left me feeling somewhat alone. It was not a good feeling, because a son should be able to go to his father for advice. When it came to my Dad, well, we just did not see eye-to-eye on anything, much less anything to do with the business.

I was lucky, though, because when I wasn't sure if what I was doing was the right way, I escaped to my Grandfather's house and asked for direction. Pop was the answer man and in the end, he always pointed me back to Frank. When Frank and I were troubled, we always knew where to find one another. Despite the fact that he was a cop, he always gave me good advice, too. I may not have liked what he said all the time, but in the end, I knew that Frank made sense in what he told me. I knew that he would never hurt me and that I could trust him to keep my secrets.

As time went on, I was becoming quite proud of him. My father loved Frank as if he were his own son, often saying, "Why can't you be like Frank?" and, "Set an example, help the community, be a good boy. Be like Frank, instead of being a gangster."

I sometimes was bothered by my father telling me to be more like Frank. I had come to see that Frank was not much different than me. He just had more patience and, at times, Frank could be equally as dangerous. He had real power in that badge and I was not sure whether he knew just how much.

No one seemed to pay much attention to that, especially my father. It was viewed that whatever Frank did, the other person deserved. Whatever I did was deemed to be poor judgment, to put it nicely. The reality was that while my father looked at me as a gangster, what he didn't know was that Frank was a gangster, too. The only difference was that he wore a badge and somehow that made it all okay.

While we were on different sides of the track, we were really one nation. I loved Frank and even Anthony too, with all my heart. That was the truth no matter what happened between us, we were all we had. We were an alliance, a trio – The Three Musketeers, a chain that could not be broken. Call it what you will, but our alliance was stronger than any of the influences around us.

CHAPTER SIXTEEN

Frank:

"Junior, get yourself ready, you have a game today," I yelled to my kid, who was always dragging his feet when I needed to be somewhere. I vaguely remember the days when I was rushing around, making my parents wait for me. "I'm on a tight schedule, so let's get going."

"All right Dad, hold on," Frankie Jr. yelled from upstairs. "I'll be down in a second. I just need to find my cleats." I chuckled because his words could have been my own, at his age.

I tried to be with the kids as much as I could when I wasn't working a second job, or overtime. Things were not easy at home. Mary was riding me all the time and not in the way I liked. It had gotten to the point where I really did not have much to say to her anymore. I just kept to myself and that seemed to bother her even more. I was stuck between a rock and a hard place.

"What's the matter with you, Frank? You're so quiet lately," Mary asked, while we waited for Frankie Jr. Mary was not really interested in why I was quiet, or what was going on in my head. All she wanted was an invitation, so that she could bitch about how terrible her life had

94

become and that it was all my fault, of course. "Frank, it's been years now and you're still doing shift work. It's getting harder for me, harder to do it all on my own. I need your help, I need you home. Don't you ever think that I need a break?" It was the same story I'd heard before. But the complaints were becoming more and more frequent.

"On your own? Are you kidding me? What do you mean, Mary? On your own? I'm out there busting my ass to give you all that you guys need. I drive a shit car and yours is new, right? We have this beautiful house that this job pays for. And now I'm here to take Frank Jr. to his game and do what a father is supposed to do. What's your problem, Mary?" I'm getting defensive, but I'll hear her out... again!

"You damn well know what my problem is. It's not about the car, Frank. I'm alone all the time. Then it's, 'Mary take the kids to the game' and 'Mary take the kids to your parents.' Or it's the holidays, where you breeze in and out and I'm left with the mess. I'm glad we have this house, but the house has only me in it, Frank. I need a friend, I need my husband. I need someone to share my life with and you're not here anymore."

I really couldn't blame her. I could see how things were slowly unraveling and why not? We weren't doing great financially and I was not home much. The job was consuming me and there was not much time for anything else. Plus, I was becoming hardened to the point where the normal things around me did not exist. Where I was once sensitive to Mary's needs, now I didn't even think about how she was doing. Some of it was because of the pressure of having to provide a home, food on the table, hell, just paying the electric bill was an issue at times. Then again, some of it was because I was just not mature enough, as a husband, to understand the needs of my wife, which really were not any different than any other women's wants and needs. As I was standing there listening to Mary and waiting for Frank Jr., I was wondering if I could make this all work, or whether it was going to explode in my face. My only hope was to get promoted and somehow hold on to my marriage long enough to figure out how to make it better.

*   *   *

Anthony:

I was watching Frank's marriage slowly fall apart and yeah, a lot of it was because we were always hustling to make a living. The shift we were on wasn't easy and I felt Mary should have given him a break, but, she was spoiled and that was because Frank put her on a pedestal when they first got married.

What Mary did not take into account was the pressure of being a mother, as well as a wife to an absent husband, she couldn't handle it. When Frank signed on to be a cop, Mary never realized just what they were getting into and time would tell to what degree it would affect their marriage.

As for me, I was smarter than Frank in that area. I knew that the married life was not for me, at least not yet anyway. I liked to play around and I was seeing one of Tommy's strippers, Vicky Rivers. It really wasn't a traditional relationship, because the bitch was naked all the time. To tell you the truth, all I wanted was to get laid and Vicky absolutely loved sex, so for us, it was a match made in heaven.

Unfortunately, Vicky got pregnant, but like I said, it was no traditional relationship and she had to make a living. Vicky had to keep that amazing body of hers intact, so, without even batting a fake eyelash, she got an abortion. Quick and dirty, it was, then right back to work on the stage. She was hardcore and knew her priorities. I could have married a girl like that, but I also knew there was no future in it.

I never told anyone about the abortion or about Vicky being pregnant. At the time, I really didn't care. It was as if I'd dodged a bullet and just kept moving on. Besides, I was not in love. I think when it's that way it's easy to just keep going. And that is what Vicky and I did. We moved on.

I was at the top of my game in the police department. I was still hoping to leave soon and the thought of joining the FBI was on my mind all the time. But, I needed to make a little money as well. The police job paid shit, so I would sometimes accompany Tommy's money to where it had to go, just to make sure it got to the right place. I didn't think I was doing anything illegal. It wasn't like I was a bag man, more like Western Union, making sure that the cash went where it was supposed to go. And with Tommy, he preferred me over his crew for the escorts because, at the end of the day, he could trust that I was not going to touch any of it. I was properly compensated, of course, so it was a win-win situation.

I was no fool, either. I knew what I was doing and yes, wanting to be in the FBI, I also knew that those ambitions could go down the drain if I got caught working for Tommy. But I wasn't getting in too deep and the money was becoming too lucrative to turn it down. No one knew anything, but I was always a little paranoid. I felt like people were watching me all the time. I knew I had to be careful, so I needed to make sure Tommy did not suck me in so far that I could not get out, especially once I joined the FBI. With the Feds, there was no halfway. You were either in all the way or out. And I was close to being in. Coincidentally, so was Frank, who was on the cusp of being promoted to detective, just at a time when he desperately needed a boost in his life.

CHAPTER SEVENTEEN

Frank:

Finally, I was promoted to detective. No more shift work, at least not like the kind I was doing, while on patrol. No more uniform either. I hated the uniform. It was like you were wearing a shit load of gear that was choking the life out of you. The bulletproof vest was the worst. Yeah, it was there to save your life, but that was only if you could survive being strapped to Kevlar and metal plates for fifteen hours a day, in the searing heat. Most people didn't know it but I only wore the vest when it was cold out. It was the perfect insulation. In the thirteen years I'd been assigned to patrol, I probably only wore it three months out of the year. Now, in the Detective Division, no more vest. Bring on the suits.

Mary was thrilled too, mostly because she saw the promotion as the answer to our marital woes. She threw a big party for me at the house and had everyone there, even the guys from my squad.

"Congratulations, Detective," Sergeant Rosa said, patting me on the back and finally giving me a big bear hug.

Ricky Rosa and I were patrolmen for many years together. He was promoted to sergeant a year or so ago and was running the major case squad.

"Thanks, Sarge. I'm glad that you were able to come to help celebrate."

Rosa replied, "Well Frank, we're back together again. Are you ready for me? Of course, you know that I'm happy to have you and when you get time, Chief Martino wants to see you."

I knew that Chief Martino was the commanding officer of the squad and it was only natural that he would want to lay down the rules for the new guy. I made a mental note to see him as soon as I could. The rest of the party went off without a hitch. Having my family and the guys from the squad there to kick off my promotion made me more confident in the future than I had ever been.

"Babe, did you like your party?" Mary asked as we were cleaning up the mess.

She started to hug me, sighing, like she had a load taken off her back. This was it, this was the time she would get her husband back.

"Where's Frankie Jr.?" I asked her, just realizing that I had not seen him for a while.

"He's with his brother outside playing and we have some time alone," Mary said, as she closed the bedroom door and stripped down to just a teddy, with garter belts. She was ready well before the party started. I was starting to sweat and it was almost like the first time I'd met her. She sure had some body on her. I dropped to my knees and kissed her everywhere. I tried to inhale her. She smelled like hot, dirty sex, almost foreign to me. She was cleaner than the board of health and I was going to eat that like it was the last supper.

Taking her by her hair, I forced her onto the bed from behind. We didn't have a lot of time, so I grabbed her hips and reached forward, slightly choking her. She came hard and I let go all over her back. The sex was incredible, for a change, and I thought that maybe we were going back to a place where our lives were fantastic, where all that mattered was Mary and me. Then I heard the kids calling me to come out to play catch. I was thinking, yeah, in a few minutes and we went at it again, this time with a little less fury and a little more loving. That's how it should be as husband and wife, right – always attracted to each other? They say people who are attracted to each other never leave one another. That's what they say, anyway.

*   *   *

Anthony:

I joined Frank in Chief Martino's office. It was strange for me to be called in with Frank. He was the one being promoted, so I was not sure why they asked me to attend. Knowing we were best friends, maybe they wanted me to pin his detective shield on him. The police department was weird like that, always having these little ceremonies, where you pinned a new badge on a guy, or a medal, or some other candy-assed shit. I am sorry for being a little cynical, but shit like these bullshit ceremonies makes me feel that way. Just give Frank his shield and let me get back to work.

The Chief started out with his little speech. "Frank, I'm very proud of you. You worked hard and deserved this promotion and you're probably wondering what you're doing here, right Crespo?"

"Well, the thought did cross my mind, Chief," I said, trying not to seem sarcastic.

"I wanted to be the first to congratulate the both of you for your promotions."

"My promotion?" I stammered, shocked at what was taking place. This was the last thing I was thinking, but hey, who am I to turn down a promotion and on the same day as Frank's?

The Chief went on, "Yes, congratulations Anthony. Effective immediately, excluding your swearing in, of course, you have also been promoted to the rank of detective."

"I really don't know what to say, Chief." I was stunned, honestly not sure how to respond.

"Say thank you. Look, I know you have been waiting to leave for the FBI. I thought maybe I could persuade you to stay. You're a damn good cop, Anthony. Why would you want to go federal? Your background doesn't even fit in with the profile of those Fed boys."

"Background? I'm not sure what you mean by that, Chief," I responded, not completely surprised by the comment, but certainly bewildered by the fact that the Chief would make it.

Frank tried to save some face for the Chief and cut in as he started to explain, "What I think the Chief means is that you're a street cop, Anthony. That's a very different thing to an FBI agent."

I looked back and forth between the two of them, not sure if I should be flattered or offended. Despite my conflict, I kept my cool. "Well, what would I be doing?" I asked. "Will I be working with Frank?"

"At some point," said the Chief. "For now, I'll keep you in narcotics, where we need you. It's what you do best and you know the players better than anyone."

"Well," Frank said, "Thanks Chief, I will meet with Ricky later."

"Ah no, Frank, no you won't. You will meet with me and Rosa regarding your new assignment. The briefing will be at fourteen-hundred."

"I guess the honeymoon is over," Frank snickered.

"Oh, and Frank, the FBI will be in attendance," the Chief added. That made my ears perk up, but I was still spinning from the recent news.

Frank just looked back at the Chief and mumbled, "The FBI?"

I took a look at Frank and the Chief and started to think about the events that had just happened. Frank and I got promoted and he got a case with the FBI. What did I get? Back to the streets, with the mutts. The Chief knew full well that I wanted to be with the Feds. Instead, he sent Frank off to them. He was patronizing me with this bullshit promotion, only to leave me right where I started. I know they thought I was "Just a street cop." Whatever! That was not going to be the end of that!

*   *   *

Frank:

So much for some time off with the new schedule. Even before the shine was off my new shield, I was being sucked into meetings and with the Chief, no less. In my first briefing with the Chief and Ricky, as soon as I walked in the door, the introductions began.

"Frank, I would like you to meet Special Agent in Charge, Fred C. Dobbs of the FBI," the Chief said, motioning to a tall, silver-haired man, who looked like he'd just stepped out of a Marlboro cigarette commercial.

"Nice to meet you, Fred, you can call me Frankie," I said, as I extended my hand. Then a familiar voice came from behind me.

"And, what can I call you?" I turned and it was none other than Agent Robert Carter. "Frank, you've come a long way since the academy," Carter said, as he took my hand, not letting go right away.

"And you followed me the whole time?" We just looked at one another until I laughed it off and finally Carter broke and started laughing too. The Chief was staring at us, unable to figure out why we looked so standoffish towards each other. But I knew, and so did Carter.

We all sat down. "Frank, you and Agent Robert Carter are assigned together, to work a fugitive case," Dobbs said.

"Fugitive case? You mean one of the warrants?"

"Not just any warrant, Frank. Your department is still looking for a known child molester who fled the country. So are we," Carter noted.

"So are we? Since when?" I asked.

Dobbs interrupted, "Since now," slamming his hand on the table, clearly not happy with my questioning of the handling of the case.

I just looked at Dobbs and thought, 'This was not going well,' and it was the Feds once more wanting to make headlines with some sensational case. I could not help myself and my smart mouth, "You mean since he's been featured on 'America's Most Wanted'?"

"Now Frank, you just got this assigned to you, I'm sure you understand we need federal cooperation to extradite this individual back into the country," the Chief explained. "We have an idea where he is, but we're not completely sure."

I was not digging this at all. This all seemed like a setup. They could have used Anthony for this. He knew the streets better than anyone and he wanted to work with the FBI. The last thing I wanted was to be mixed up with some headline-grabbing Feds.

"Isn't there another detective working the case?" I asked, with the hopes that maybe I can get out of this. "Wouldn't Anthony be better off working this case? I just got to this unit and there must be people better at this than I am. I was looking to settle into major cases, not chase fugitives."

Dobbs laughed, "I can feel the love already."

Chief Martino said, "You have your orders, Frank. There's a lot of follow-up that needs to be done to confirm his location. Now get to it and I don't want to hear any shit about you not getting along with these guys. This is a team effort, so work with the team. Got it?" He gave me that famous look of his that only Kevin could do. It was the kind you knew better not to question.

"Yeah, I got it," I glared back at him.

"What did you say Frank?" the Chief demanded.

"I mean, yes Sir."

ALLIANCE

Dobbs and Carter got up, thanked the Chief and left the room. Carter turned towards me as he was leaving, "I'll see you tomorrow, Frankie. Lunch at the Saloon?"

I just stared at him and started walking out of the room.

"Frank!" the Chief yelled towards me, "Come back here." I turned around and gave him a look, which said, 'Please, not now.'

"Close the door," the Chief ordered. "You want to tell me what that was all about?"

"Do you really want to know, Sir?" I tried to say respectfully, knowing that he really did not want to know. He was trying to stay on top of the jackpot that was brewing right under his nose.

"Frank, part of being in major cases is cooperating with all outside agencies. All of them. I know you're used to dealing with Terry Robinson, but your plate just got a lot heavier. Make it work. I trust everything will work out fine. Carter is a decorated agent and I've done a lot of work with Dobbs over the years, mostly in organized crime. They're not bad guys."

I didn't respond, I just stared at him. My silence would unnerve most people, but the Chief was a hard egg to crack. I just knew if I said anything else, it would only start shit I didn't want to get into. I went to leave again, but the Chief interrupted that, "Oh, and Frank, Carter is as straight as they come."

THE BEGINNING

"And?"

"That's all."

CHAPTER
EIGHTEEN

Anthony:

It had been several months since my promotion and nothing had really changed. Robert Carter was working with Frank and here I was, right where I'd started, except, just with a higher rank and a few more dollars in my pocket. One of the downsides was working with Terry Robinson. If I had to work one more case with him, I was going to shoot that mother-fucker.

I met Terry in his jurisdiction to discuss an up-and-coming street gang that was making waves among the other factions. The crew was led by the DeSantos brothers and I was looking to Terry to see if he had any intelligence on this new group and what they had in store for the rival gangs.

"Terry, what do you have on Angel DeSantos?" I asked him, knowing that what was coming next was more of his wise-ass remarks. I swear he did that shit just to piss me off. I thought he just wanted me to punch him in the mouth, so he could go back and cry about how he couldn't work with me. Maybe because he thinks I am a Neanderthal or something.

"What's the matter, Crespo? Couldn't pick a better place than this park to meet?" And there it was, the start of the crap all over again.

"What the fuck? Did you want me to take you to dinner? Maybe kiss you on the lips and tell you I love you? It's a fucking meet, so let's get on with it. I've got things to do." Without giving me the answers, Terry came back with yet another stupid question. His bullshit was really pissing me off and lending credence to the fact that I really couldn't stand him.

"What's your interest in the DeSantos brothers?" Terry asked smugly.

"Okay, um nothing? I just like saying the name, because I am Italian and it sounds good rolling off my tongue. You stupid bastard!" Now I'm pissed. He can't get to the point and he's wasting my time. I can't wait to get away from this job. "You know what Terry, I get it, you don't know a fucking..."

That was when Terry stopped me in my tracks and decided to actually say something worthwhile. "Angel DeSantos is a self-made man. He deals mostly in crack cocaine and doesn't really have a place he calls home. He's also very green in the business. He operates between both our jurisdictions, but mostly in mine and why?" Terry stopped right there as if he expected me to give him the answer. But the reality was, we both knew the answer. I knew full well he was taking his time to tell me because he knew it was going to get under my skin. And right on cue, there it was. "And why," Terry parrots, "Because of one very difficult obstacle, who, I believe, you are familiar with. Just one crazy, vicious maniac, who goes by the name of Tommy DePriati. Do you know him, Anthony?"

I put my hand up to stop him. "Okay, that's enough," I tell Terry. "I get it. But I'm here to talk about DeSantos and his crew, who have become an issue for me. Not Tommy DePriati."

"DeSantos?" Terry replied. "Or, DePriati, which is it?"

"I can see this is going nowhere, Terry." I was starting to raise my voice. His rhetoric and accusations had me concerned about his priorities.

He came back at me, "Nowhere? Are you kidding me? You are going to stand there and really say nowhere to me. You want me to ignore DePriati but focus on DeSantos, a guy you want me to help you nail with my informant. Is that what you want? I see where your focus is and I know why. You want me to explain this to you?" Terry kept going, "Nowhere you say? Nowhere is a word that means not happening."

I'd had enough at that point, lost my cool and started making a scene right there in the park. If his rant was not enough, then that fucker Terry was playing like Webster's dictionary, giving me the definition of the word.

"Enough!" I screamed. "Alright, I get it, you don't like me and I don't like you. If you don't want to work with me, just say so. Get the fuck away from me and I will make this case without you."

At that point, I could see Terry was starting to freak out and that sarcastic grin was being erased from his face. I think he realized that if I did this without him, it would not look good back at his headquarters. 'Terry Robinson, the prick that could not work with anyone, especially a newly appointed detective, who needed all the help he can get.' Yeah, that would not go down well with his bosses. I could see that I had his attention now and that the wheels were turning in his head. I could almost read his mind, knowing that he was thinking of his professional survival and that took precedence over his hatred for me.

"Look, all I need is for you to get one of my under-covers an introduction to that cocksucker, DeSantos and I'll take care of the rest," I told Terry as reasonably as I could, now that he had calmed down.

Terry sighed. "An introduction, that's all, right?"

"Yes, please," I responded, biting my tongue in an effort not to escalate things back to a full-blown war with Terry.

He then started walking away, before turning to me and saying, "I'll see what I can do."

Terry just solidified the reasons why I couldn't stand him. He was constantly bringing Tommy into the conversation every time we worked a case together. I knew that things were going to get complicated, and right now, I did not need complicated.

CHAPTER NINETEEN

Frank:

I had been working with Robert Carter for a while now and we were getting close to finishing our assignment. Chief Martino wasn't kidding about how straight that guy was, but everyone had a flaw and Carter was no exception. I guess I wasn't the only one having issues at home because of this job. It came to my attention and also to my utmost surprise that Carter had a fetish. Yes, you heard me – a fetish. It wasn't anything obscene, or something that would kill the guy's career if people found out. It was that he liked women. You see Carter did not simply like women, he adored them: Blondes, brunettes, redheads, fat, skinny, big breasts, small, it did not matter. He loved them all and where best to find these women than in the very kind of strip clubs that Tommy operated. Maybe that was why Carter had such an interest in me right out of the gate. Maybe he thought I knew about him and the girls, and more importantly, that Tommy knew, too. You're probably wondering how I came to find out, right? Even Carter himself had to eventually give it up. We started playing softball together and he began talking more and more to me in the relaxed atmosphere. He let his guard down some, opening up a bit, but in a riddle-like way.

"Good game, Kid," I used to say to him on the field. See, I started calling Carter, "The Kid." It was because he loved Gary Carter of the Mets, right down to wearing his number when we played.

"It was all right," Carter replied.

"Looks like we may make the playoffs," I said to him. "You think you'll still be in town long enough for us to finish them?"

"I should be," Carter replied. "Sooner or later though I have to get back to my wife, Frank, or I won't have one anymore."

And that was when Carter opened up about compensating for the downtime in strange cities. It was all about his affection for pretty women, preferably the cooperative, naked kind. I wasn't born yesterday, so I knew just what he meant and for now, I was going to keep it under my hat. You know, a little nugget that could prove useful on a rainy day and right now, it was all sunny skies. The only thing that sucked about the conversation was that Carter was too smart for his own good and knew my weakness, too.

"And, how are you and Mary getting along?" he asked, deflecting the attention. "The long hours, this new job, and now you being a detective, can't be making her very happy, especially since you're out of the house more than ever."

I just looked at him and really did not know what to say. He had me there and I'm sure there was something he knew as well and sure enough that came out of his mouth, too. I just looked at him and shook my head in disbelief. It was strange the way he asked, like he had walked down the same path before. "Oh, one other thing. I would be careful around Paige Brown. She's a man hunter and I heard she's gunning for you. Oh, wait, you already knew that, didn't you? And, um, Mary knows too, right?" Carter chuckled a little at the end there.

Great! With everything else that was going on, now I had to worry about Paige, especially since Mary once caught us in the bar together. Nothing happened, but hey, Paige is a looker and I am only human. The bigger question is, how did this prick know all about me and Mary and Paige, at all? I guess Carter and I may be two peas in a pod. But even so, I was not going to say anything that let this FBI snoop get something over on me. There is just too much to risk at this point and as long as we both had our cards on the table I would be able to deal with whatever he thought he had on me.

CHAPTER
TWENTY

Tommy:

"Good afternoon, Thomas," Dobbs said, as he strolled into my place as if he owned it.

"I don't remember inviting you into my bar."

"Come on, Thomas, why all the hard feelings? It's not like I've locked you up or anything. Well, not yet, anyway," Dobbs added sarcastically.

I was having a bad day and the last thing I needed was for the FBI to visit me. As it was, that prick, Fred C. Dobbs, had been a thorn in Grandpa's side for years, back to when he was a field agent. And now he was a supervisor. Either way, he was still a first class ball-buster. The bigger question, though, why was he here? I hoped it had nothing to do with my cousin. The last thing I needed was a bunch of agents putting me under a microscope through my family. This could be the start of my worst nightmare.

Dobbs continued, "No need to worry, Tom. I only came by to say hello to an old friend."

"And you could just as quickly say goodbye and turn around to leave. Oh, and don't get any crazy ideas. We're not friends, and we will never be friends. So just do whatever it is, you have to do and go on your way."

Even though I was trying to get Dobbs to leave, he was in no hurry to go. I realized why when the next thing I heard was, "So is he here or not?" and I turned around and saw Robert Carter approaching Dobbs. What else could go wrong with my day? Needless to say, I was not happy about both of these guys paying me a visit, but I wasn't going to let them get the best of me, at least not that day.

"Figures, first Dobbs and now you, Carter, you rigid fuck. The only thing straighter than you is my dick." I began to pace, looking back and forth between Carter and Dobbs. I was not going to let this pass without letting dear old Bobby Carter know that I was onto his act and knew exactly what to say to blow up his spot. I looked at both of them and let it out, "I see you haven't been a stranger to my establishments, Bobby, now have you? Which one is your favorite, again? Oh, no need to tell me because I can tell where you have been, by the tips you leave the girls. If you even leave a tip, you cheap fuck."

Dobbs glanced quickly at Carter, in disappointment. Not because of what Carter did, but that he put the credibility of the agency at risk. The bigger issue was that it also showed weakness and that was something very few people ever saw in Carter. You see, you couldn't have any cracks in the pavement for someone like me to squeeze through. I made it my business to find the kinks in the armor of those that opposed me. And then I used them to neutralize my enemies and those two fucks were enemy's number one and number two.

"Look, Thomas, I'm not here to hear about your fabled beliefs regarding my agents. And, I can't help it if some of them have a hormone problem. I'm only interested to know if they broke the law." Dobbs glanced at Carter, nodding towards him and said, "Because, if they did, I would be the first to come down on them like holy hell."

The room went quiet for a second and out of the back office, a silhouette of a man emerged from the darkness. "I know that smell. It smells like a cheap fuck." Out of the shadows came Grandpa, shaking his head in disbelief.

Within a second, Dobbs and Grandpa were face-to-face for the first time since Dobbs tried to charge him under the RICO Act. Carter said, "Well if it isn't old 'Sally Balls' himself. How're things, Mr. DePriati?"

"Things, Bobby? I'm not going to speak to you, you're even less relevant than he is," Grandpa said, motioning towards Dobbs.

I knew better than to say anything. In this business, you learn fast that when people are talking, you listen, especially when those people are the likes of Sal DePriati. Grandpa used to say, 'You'll never know what you heard if you never listened to what was said.' Sounds poetic, right? But in our business, it could mean the difference between life and death.

"Bobby, pay no mind to Mr. DePriati here," Dobbs said to Carter. "You see, our dear friend 'Sally Balls' could become insignificant at any moment of the day. In fact…"

"Agent Dobbs," Grandpa interrupted, "Do you have a search warrant? Do you have an arrest warrant? 'Cause if you don't, I suggest you have a drink, on me and then vacate the premises."

Things were getting heated and Grandpa was glaring at Dobbs with his famous death stare. If Dobbs wasn't a Fed, I could assure you that he would never have left the bar, well, not through the front door anyway. It became apparent that I wasn't the only one who felt Grandpa's wrath coming to the boil. Benny must have sensed the tension too and emerged from the back room and made his way between both agents, leaving Dobbs and Carter surrounded.

It had turned into a Mexican-standoff, with everyone waiting for the other to flinch. While Grandpa and I both understood the code about not killing cops, Benny was another story. But to his credit, Benny held his ground and waited.

Dobbs felt the tension too and knew the only way to handle it was to lighten the mood and back down a little. So, he broke the silence. "Nope, I don't have a warrant for your arrest and I certainly don't have a search warrant. They go hand-in-hand, ya know? But sooner or later… oh, never mind. You still have that Irish whiskey I used to drink?"

Grandpa could see that Dobbs did not want the situation to get out of hand and he knew there would be another time to deal with him, so he took the high road, for the moment anyway.

"You mean the one with the dust on it?" Grandpa asked Dobbs, with half a smile on his face. Dobbs nodded and Grandpa motioned to the bartender. "Hey Randy, pour these gentlemen a glass of that bottle up there, the one with the 'X' on it."

Randy grabbed the bottle and poured two glasses, neat. Grandpa handed them to the agents, looked them both in the eyes, saying, "It's on me."

Dobbs grabbed the drink and sipped half of it, not even wincing at the effects of the aged whiskey. "Ahhhhh… now that's some good shit."

I couldn't help but chuckle. "Why don't you take a bath in it, Dobbs? It'll smell better than that cheap shit you're wearing now."

Grandpa looked at me in disgust. "Tommy, did I ask you to speak?"

That was the first time I had ever felt embarrassed since I took over for Grandpa. But I knew he was right. It wasn't the right moment or time.

"Apologize to Agent Dobbs, Thomas," Grandpa ordered.

"And Carter, too?" I asked.

"No, just Agent Dobbs will do."

I walked out and as I passed Dobbs, murmured, "Enjoy your fucking drink. There's my apology."

Grandpa laughed, looked at Dobbs and said, "Kids these days, eh? They'll be the death of ya."

*   *   *

Frank:

I met Carter at the station with Dobbs. Our time together was close to an end. We had briefings from time to time, but this was one of the few occasions where Dobbs attended.

"Well, Frank," Dobbs said. "Your work with Carter on this case was exemplary. The target has been located and picked up by Interpol, so our role in this is pretty much finished."

"So, I'm thinking that means the subject will be extradited to Miami, right?" Carter said, giving me a look that meant more was coming.

So I took the bait and asked, "Well, he should be, but what the fuck, Kid? It sounds like your trying to wrangle up a trip to the sunshine state."

"Come on Frank, why not? We earned it."

"Hold on, you two," Dobbs cut in. "Only one of you is going to Miami, so get it out of your heads. There are no free vacations on this job, especially for you Carter. I can read your mind and it's flashing bikini girls loud and clear."

I had to smirk at that because Dobbs had Carter pegged perfectly and all I could do was mutter, "That figures."

"Well, I'm spent," said Dobbs, as he stretched his arms out in exhaustion.

With Dobbs done for the day, Carter turned to me and asked, "You heading home?"

"No, I'm gonna stop for a drink first and unwind a little."

"Unwind again, huh? Not healthy Frank. Booze every night is just the start of a life of disappointments," he said, very matter-of-factly.

"Yeah, that's true, but it is a whole lot safer than a broken condom, if you know what I mean Bobby-boy," I smirked at him, punching him lightly in the arm.

"You're a real asshole Frank," he replied, a little more seriously than I intended.

"Hey, I'm just kidding, have a nice night doing whatever it is you plan to do."

I think I pissed Carter off a little and maybe rubbed some salt in the wound with the condom remark, but hey, fuck him, if he can't take a joke.

As I walked away, I received a call from Tommy. "Hey cousin, what's up?" I asked.

"Come by, I want to talk for a few," was all he said before he hung up. I was surprised at his curt statement, but despite my better judgment, I stopped by. It worked in my favor anyway since I needed a drink and by seeing Tommy at the same time, I wouldn't have to go too far.

"You rang?" I asked, as I hugged him from behind and planted a kiss on his cheek. I was excited that my first big case was over and it went well.

"Nice to see ya happy, Frank." Tommy leaned over and hugged me back.

Why not? I'm almost done with Carter and Dobbs and it was clear sailing from here, I thought.

"Usual, Frank?" asked Trevor, who was one of Tommy's two regular bartenders.

"Absolutely, Trev." I couldn't wait to get a sip. You gotta love a bartender as considerate as Trev. The guy was hired by my grandfather as a favor to a friend. He had no bartending skills coming in, so what did he do? He made a list and posted it daily of all the tasks he needed to do for the day. We used to bust his balls and call it a 'Trevor List.' But, it worked and Trev became one top-notch bartender and it was all because of the list. He knew what everyone drank and provided a quick pour long before you even warmed the barstool.

But, back to Tommy. He looked serious. I could tell something was up. Trevor, who always bullshitted with me, walked away, real fast. I looked at my cousin and there it was; the smirk. That little smile that always gave Tommy away and I knew something was going on.

"What happened, Tommy?" I asked.

He was drinking scotch and he sipped it a couple of times, making me wait, kind of like an actor using a pause for effect. Then, in that 'I hate you as a cop' voice, said, "You wanna tell me why the Irish Lone Ranger and Carter were in my bar today harassing me?" Grandpa had coined the nickname "Irish Lone Ranger" for Dobbs and I hadn't heard anyone call him that in a while. But rather than dwell on that, all I could do was wonder why they were visiting Tommy. Why would Carter risk being seen in there while on the job?

"They were?"

"No... I just said that 'cause I like to say their names," Tommy replied sarcastically, shifting his weight towards me.

"All right, take it easy Tommy." I put my hand on his shoulder, trying to calm him down.

Tommy shrugged my hand off of him and raised his voice. "Fuck you, Frank! Fuck you! You and creep-o-Crespo, you two joining the police department with a background like ours, never ceases to amaze me. But why? Because you couldn't be like me?"

Tommy was drunk. He wasn't making complete sense but I have to admit, I was puzzled myself. I had no clue why Dobbs and Carter would come to see Tommy, but more so, why today of all days, when we had just mopped up a big case. I had just left them and neither Dobbs nor Carter said anything about meeting Tommy, or Grandpa.

"I really don't know, Tommy. I really don't. What did they want?"

"Well, now that you ask, cousin, the answer is, not much. That was the weird part. See, Grandpa was here, too, and after he embarrassed me, they left," Tommy explained, clenching his teeth as he did.

"I'll look into it, Tommy. But I can't promise anything. They didn't tell me they were here and I can't make a big deal about something I'm not supposed to know happened."

My cousin stood up and he could barely walk. He was tanked. He leaned into me and said, "You better and I don't care what it takes. You find out why those scumbags are suddenly on me. Better than that, you better get rid of them."

I looked at him and said, "I'll see what I can do," which turned out to be the wrong thing to say because Tommy was getting really excited and was about to lose it. He was mad and getting to a boiling point.

He turned towards me and began to jab his finger into my chest saying, "You, you better not forget what I told you. Get rid of those bums, or…"

But, before he could finish the sentence, he rolled off of me and staggered out of the bar. Either he thought I understood the threat or realized it was a mistake to start poking me. See, cousin or not, Tommy was not going to treat me the way he treated his crew. Both of us had an ego and if he started pushing me, it would most likely end up in a brawl.

Tommy was upset that the Feds harassed him a little. I, too, was curious as to why they chose to pay him a visit. Up until that point, my years in the police department had flashed by without a single inquiry regarding my relationship with Tommy. There was nothing in my work that pointed me even remotely in his direction, despite the awkward introduction to Carter at the academy years ago. I needed to find out what had caused this to become an issue all of a sudden.

The next morning, I ran into Dobbs in the office. It struck me, how was I going to ask about this? I really didn't want to stir any shit up and I just couldn't say out of the clear blue sky, 'Hey Dobbs, why are you and Carter harassing my cousin?'

All I could muster was, "Hey, Dobbs, packing up huh?" which was weak, given all I had to ask him.

"Yup," Dobbs replied. "I'm leaving and Carter will be out of here soon, too."

"Did you enjoy your visit with us?" I asked, hoping to warm him up.

"Yeah, I did. I even managed to have a couple of drinks yesterday."

"Really? Did you have a good time?"

The room was empty and he was standing in front of me like we were gonna draw down on each other. I could see a questionable look on his face like he was going to unload on me and I would not have to ask a single question. But instead, he just played coy and that made the entire event even worse. "You could say that, Frank. I got the chance to see some old friends."

"That's always nice," I smiled, waiting for him to go on about being at Tommy's bar. But Dobbs stopped there and headed towards the door. Before he stepped out, he gave me a look and said, "You're a real good cop, Frank, try to stay that way."

Startled, I just stared at him. I knew what Dobbs meant, but I really expected more from him. I didn't understand why he didn't bring Tommy up, or the reason he and Carter went to the bar. I guess in the long run it did not matter. He went to the bar, said his piece and left.

ALLIANCE

No one was arrested and no one got killed thank goodness. I would have to leave it be for the time being, but wasn't sure it would end there.

CHAPTER
TWENTY-ONE

Tommy:

Business was good and with the addition of Benny, everyone was staying in line. However, the added business meant that Scopa had his hands full, so I allowed him to hire a young assistant to help with the additional things that needed to get done. Scopa wanted someone he could groom as an enforcer. In the meantime, I wanted him to use whoever he hired to learn how to earn. After all, I wasn't made of money and hiring on extra guys meant that they would have to pay their way.

We settled on a guy called Vinny Manzo. He was young, maybe too young for what Scopa would have him do. But I would have Benny keep an eye on him just in case he got in over his head. As it was, he was a ballsy little bastard and seemed to have no fear. But even still, there was always a risk when you hired someone from outside the family. I wanted to make sure that there was not going to be any exposure with Vinny on board. Really, it was more than that though.

Vinny was not up on who and what we were. He thought he answered to Scopa and no one else. The other thing about Vinny that bothered me, was that the women liked him a bit too much for my taste. Too much fraternizing, way too friendly for a guy who was supposed to be a hammer. However, it was too early to tell how he would turn out, so I would let Scopa keep him around for a while, as long as he stayed in line.

"Vinny," Scopa called to his young recruit. "Come meet the boss."

Vinny replied, "The boss? I thought you were the boss. Who's this guy?"

Benny leaned into him and whispered, almost as if it were a warning, "Yes, our boss. Our boss, you idiot!"

Vinny just shook his head, with a look of disbelief. Then he took my hand and instead of giving one of those grips of respect, he was just limp. You know, like a wet dishrag, almost like it was too much for him to shake my hand like a man. Here I am, Don DePriati, a kingpin, leader of a crew, and huge money-maker for the family, and this kid looked at me like I was part of the wallpaper. I was going to have to have a conversation with Scopa about Vinny. I needed to know more about this kid. But for now, there was business that needed handling. We were in Ron's and it had a nice sized parking lot and that was a good place to stash this kid. So I turned to Scopa and said, "Send Vinny to the lot to park cars. We have visitors coming."

"Vinny, go in the back lot, do the meet and greet and park the cars," Scopa directed.

THE BEGINNING

"Park cars?" Vinny said, challenging our orders.

"No, fuck them in the ass and then park them," Scopa barked, running out of patience with him. "Get going you fuck and don't give me any more of your lip."

Vinny walked off, staring Scopa down as if he were a nobody. Scopa looked at me and said, "I know, I know. He has an attitude problem and I'm working on it. Trust me, Tommy, he has a lot of uses."

"Uses for what?" I scoffed. "For who? For you, maybe?" I asked again. I could not believe what I was hearing here.

"No, Tommy, of course not, for the family. He'll be of good use to the family."

Scopa always knew how to defuse my anger and his go-to line was about the family, as he raised his glass to toast. But for one second there, something didn't feel right. I looked at Scopa and there was a feeling that maybe he and Vinny would not last. Scopa was way too ambitious, slightly misguided but with lots of balls. I could see that I might have to chop them off somewhere down the line.

Anyway, I would have to settle the Vinny situation with him later. For now, I had issues to settle with a new group, the DeSantos brothers. This crew was young and eager. They were pushing drugs on 48th Street, which I didn't mind so much. I mean everyone has got to eat, right? As long as they stayed on 48th Street and minded their manners. But that wasn't necessarily happening.

Angel DeSantos was the leader of the outfit. I sent for him to discuss territorial issues. He had a history with Benny and it wasn't a positive encounter. In fact, Benny almost lost an eye sending a message to him for his old boss in Florida. Angel's cousin took a hot iron to Benny's face. It was so bad from what I heard, Benny was knocked out cold. Basically, Benny was caught off guard. Believe me, that was not classic Benny Costa and it was a rare occurrence. Supposedly, the DeSantos' took a picture of his face and it circulated a bit. Shortly after that, Angel's cousin disappeared. No surprise there. Did they really think that they could try to hit Benny and get away with it? Their biggest mistake was leaving him alive. They should have killed him. It would have been safer because guys like Benny didn't forget. It was supposed to be business, guess he made it personal and in the end, a statement had to be made. In this case, it was Angel's cousin who got the message. They were not the best of friends and I didn't feel like fucking refereeing anyone, so I hoped Angel kept his place.

"Angel DeSantos, nice to meet you," he said and put his hand out to Vinny, who was the first to confront him out in the parking lot.

Vinny just looked at him and said, "Yeah you are. Now I know."

Angel tossed his keys at Vinny who let them fall to the ground. Then when Angel walked by Vinny, he could not help but bite back. "I'll be back in an hour, so keep it warm for me. I will be sure to tell my guys to see the valet when I am ready to pick it up."

Vinny replied as he picked up the keys, "Sure thing, cock-sucker."

Angel had two other members of his group with him. I guess he felt he needed backup or something. Maybe he thought he was going to get hit. Who knows?

"Tommy D, great to see you," Angel bellowed.

I just had to smile and shake my head. "I'm glad you could come, Angel. Have a seat. Benny, take Angel's men up front for drinks and entertainment while Scopa and I speak with him."

Benny walked by Angel and just ignored him. I was a bit surprised. Whatever, it was better off that way. It was not a meeting for violence. It was a sit-down and I had a point to get across and did not need a war to break out right there in the bar.

Once we were all settled, Angel said, "So, I'm here, what can I do for you?"

"No, my friend, it is not what you can do for me, but what you aren't going to do, going forward," I told him, making sure that there was no confusion about what was going on here today. But apparently, there was a language problem because Angel acted like he '*no habla ingles.*'

"I don't follow you," Angel responded, acting as if he did not get the point, or even know what the fuck I was talking about. So I had to spell it out for the fucker.

"Your business is doing well. You're dealing up on 48th Street. I couldn't help but notice that you're dealing beyond that as well. Look at you Angel, all fancy, nice clothes. You're having a great run, right?"

And even before I finished the last of my sentence, Scopa couldn't help himself and leaned in close to Angel and in a threatening manner said, "Looks that way to me, too. You seem to be doing quite well for yourself, Angel. A hundred percent."

Angel just looked at me, searching for words that could not come out of his mouth. His face drained of its color. Maybe he thought he was going to get whacked right there and then.

Scopa went on to explain our position about Angel's new-found success.

"You're trespassing. Plain and simple. Do you *'comprende'* that?" Scopa asked.

"Trespassing?" Angel repeated. "How am I trespassing?"

"Not all the time," I told him, trying to be gentle, but wanting to get my point across. "Angel, for me, it has been too many times and more than once means you are disrespecting me and my family."

Angel, getting nervous, stammered, "Tommy, the border, she has thin lines. It's easy for my people to make a mistake now and then. I'm not trying to disrespect you."

"Maybe," I replied. "But that answer is not gonna work for me. I am not interested in blurred lines, or how blind you may, or may not be when it comes to where you belong."

Angel cut in, "Things are tough. The times, they get rough here and there, especially since your cousin and Crespo have been..."

"My cousin," I screamed.

"Well yeah, your cousin, you know…"

I interrupted Angel again. "Mentioning Frank could be hazardous to your health," I said, as I pointed my finger at him, letting him know what the message was without saying it. Look, I was not happy that Frank was a cop, more so a Detective now. Angel mentioning him to me in any fashion wouldn't be tolerated. But Angel was not stupid either and he quickly knew how to back up and make nice.

"Hey, hey, easy Tommy," he said. "Frank's doing what he's got to do. It's very noble that he's a cop out there protecting the community against the bad guys. I was just saying sometimes we trip over your territory by accident. It's hard to stay out of Frank's way and the same goes for that cocksucker, Robinson. In case you're not paying attention, they're grooming some kid, Vincent Toro, right out of the academy, straight into narcotics and that can mean more trouble for me and you. That's all I am saying, no disrespect intended."

I looked at Scopa. I didn't have to say anything. Scopa knew it was the look of, 'Why didn't I know about this guy Vincent Toro?' I turned back to Angel, "You have 48th Street and that's it. You get one free pass. You trip up again and I will tax you. You walk over the line after that, I don't care if it's to avoid a fucking train coming at you, expect the worst."

"I get it," Angel yelled with disgust. "I get it," he repeated in a lower voice.

"Great, then we all agree. Scopa, escort Angel to the front, make sure he has a good time and then show him to his car."

"Will do, boss," Scopa replied.

They both started walking away. "Oh, and Angel, watch out for the potholes in my parking lot. Some are so big you could drown in one and never be seen again."

He just looked back at me and almost ran into a wall. I couldn't help but laugh. Yeah, I think I got his attention. Thing is, that guy was not scared of anything. But today was different. He knew he'd crossed the line and that it could have cost him. I think Angel was just surprised he made it out of the room alive.

CHAPTER TWENTY-TWO

Scopa:

After that whole ordeal with Angel was over, things fell back into their natural order. Tommy and I were starting to gel and he was getting comfortable with me being by his side. But I'm Scopa and playing second fiddle did not sit well with me. I was used to making calculated moves and, as they say, a leopard doesn't change his spots.

I played poker for a living, with the idea that I would always make the best moves at the right time. I mean, my nick-name wasn't "G-Money" for nothing. After our meeting with DeSantos, I had to admit I was intrigued with the way Angel was making money. I also knew that if I even thought about dealing drugs, these guineas would have no problem giving me the death penalty. But money is money and like in poker, it was all how you played the hand. One night I was talking to someone who cared very little for the mob rule about not dealing drugs, but it was just a talk.

"Grace, honey, I'll take a Tito's vodka, seltzer and a splash of cranberry," I said, after hitting her with a wink and a nod.

I made the gesture because Flatts had just stepped up and took the stool next to me. Flatts loved women. Unfortunately, he had communication issues when he tried to talk to them. He was always at a loss for the right things to say and sometimes it just came out all wrong.

"That barmaid is some piece of ass. Isn't she?" Flatts noted, right on cue.

"Better talk to her now, if you like her. I heard she was becoming a stewardess or some shit," I told him, putting the pressure on him to chat her up.

"Maybe later," Flatts mumbled, bowing out of contention for the barmaid's attention even before getting started. In truth, I wasn't there to break Flatts' balls. I needed something else from him.

"What's your take on the business Angel is generating?" I asked Flatts.

"Well, I think it's spiffy, just spiffy," Flatts replied, taking a couple of swigs of his stout in-between. I didn't have time for his nonsense.

"English, Flatts. In English, please," I demanded.

"For fuck's sakes Scopa. You know I'm not going there, so don't even ask me."

"Going where? I didn't say anything about going anywhere. I just wanted your take on Angel and what kind of cash he's raking in."

Flatts gave me that look like he wanted to say something before I stopped him.

"Don't answer. All I'm saying is that it would be nice to get a piece of the pie. There's enough room out there for everyone." What the hell? Did I have to spell out everything for this guy?

Flatts gave me the stare down, before taking a long pull on his drink, saying, "You guys have rules, some very old rules. These are the kind of rules that are not to be broken. If you think…"

I saw this was not going the way I had hoped and stopped Flatts in mid-sentence. I got real close to his face, so he knew I wasn't playing any games, "Did I say I was gonna break a rule. Did I? You know what Flatts, just forget about it."

"Look, I only want some friendly conversation," Flatts replied. "Scopa, please understand that I'm only here because of the gratuity of Enrico DeEsso and Sally Balls. My gratitude extends to them, hence to Tommy DePriati. I'm not looking to have any issues and in case you don't know it, the walls have ears and I'm not talking."

With that Flatts got up and took his drink, leaving me there on the bar stool to talk to myself. Fortunately, I wasn't alone long, because from behind me came the familiar voices of two women entering the bar. It was two lovelies, Tina Romano and Paige Brown.

Tina was the sister of Jackie Romano, who had just started working for Tommy as a dancer. All three of them would have drinks, from time to time at The Saloon.

"Hello, little lady," I said to Tina. She was a fine-ass blonde and I couldn't resist talking to her after that bullshit conversation with Flatts, "And Paige, how are you doing?"

"Well, Scopa, very well and thanks for not calling me a lady, fuck-nuts," Paige responded.

Even though my focus was on Tina, she ignored me at first. Tina had known Tommy for a while and was friends with his fiancée, Samantha. After Samantha's disappearance, she had nothing but anger for Tommy and anyone associated with him didn't fare any better either. However, I had to give it the old college try, not that I went to college or anything.

"Paige, you gonna introduce me to Tina?"

"Tina, this is Scopa. There I'm done. You're introduced," Paige said, not hiding her disdain.

Paige then looked over at the front door and saw Jameson walking in. He came over and slipped his hand down her back, touching the top of her ass and she knew what that meant.

Paige said, "Saved by the bell."

"Bell?" Jameson laughed, "Ain't nothing here shaped like a bell, honey."

Paige laughed at Jameson's comment.

"Well, you two have fun. See ya later," Jameson nodded, as he and Paige headed to his favorite stall in the Men's Room.

"I hate when she acts like a whore," Tina said.

Surprised by her comment, I told her, "Come on, They've been messing with each other for a while now. You know nature has a right to take its course, even if it's with a scumbag cop like Jameson."

"I guess," Tina said.

"So, can I buy you a drink?"

Slapping her hand on the bar, she replied, "Why not?"

"Grace, two vodkas, neat."

"How the fuck do you even know what I drink?" Tina asked.

"I pay attention, which sometimes is a sign of a great listener," I said coyly.

"Yeah alright, so you have a good line of bullshit," she smiled.

Me and Tina talked for over two hours and thankfully Paige never came back. I guessed that she left with Jameson, leaving Tina behind.

142

"Well, it's getting late," Tina finally offered. "I have to be up early for work tomorrow."

"You live nearby?" I asked.

"Yup, within walking distance."

"How about I walk with you? Ya know these streets can get dangerous."

"I'll tell you what," she answered. "You can walk me home Mr. Card player and that's it… this time."

"Done, deal me in."

So I was in heaven. I had made some headway with Tina, even if it just meant walking her home.

*　　　*　　　*

Tommy:

Scopa was so wrapped up in this girl he didn't see us watching him. I chuckled a little, "I don't know if I like that."

"Why Tommy, you jealous?"

"No, it's not that Benny. I just don't like gatherings of people who don't like me."

"What? Scopa?" Benny asked.

"Never mind," I said and just walked off as Benny finished his cigarette.

As I walked away, I could see Scopa bending down to kiss Tina and then put his hand on her ass. She slapped Scopa good, right across the face. Benny tossed his cigarette to the ground, disgusted as he walked off mumbling, "What a real fucking Romeo."

CHAPTER TWENTY-THREE

Frank:

It had been a few years since my promotion and I was busy all the time. Detective Frank Risi had a great ring to it and I was loving every minute of it. My skills were as sharp as a tack and got better with every case I worked. However, it wasn't a total picnic and the responsibilities and pressures of working major case were really getting to me. What made it worse was that there were very few people I could talk to about it. And it wasn't just me, because even Terry was starting to break. We worked in separate jurisdictions but had the same problems. I had just finished a drug case with him and Anthony and it wasn't pretty. I really wasn't into narcotics, which was Anthony's bag and he wasn't digging it that much either anymore. He was tired of it all, tired of the dealers, the long hours and we were not really making a difference anyway. Anthony was getting bitter and couldn't give a fuck about anything or anyone.

As it was, we were working a CI together on a large drug operation. It took over three months just to get a buy into the place. The house was part of a townhouse complex, where each unit was attached and had its own garage, which seemed to have a lot of activity in and around it. The group was affecting both jurisdictions and I was a bit surprised Anthony was involved like he was. He was eager, but it was odd because he really didn't care anymore. So it puzzled me why he wanted to be mixed up in this case.

These guys were pushing Special K and Ecstasy. The communities where they were being sold were terribly impacted by it. The children were getting hooked and once they were addicted and ran out of money, they did anything they could to get the drugs. Unfortunately, that included violence and fencing stolen property. The investigation ran through the holidays and even on Christmas Eve, kids were breaking into homes, stealing gifts right out from under the tree. It was awful, and if we didn't do something soon, it was only going to get worse.

We had to get into the house and since we could not get an introduction done through the CI, we came up with another way to do it. You could call it genius or just plain luck. The target in the investigation was this guy, Ramirez, who just happened to be outside of his house. So we used an undercover to act as if he was being chased by the police. He ran to the end of the cul-de-sac and approached Ramirez in a panic.

"Can you help me? The police are fucking chasing me," he screamed to Ramirez.

Ramirez had his garage door partially opened and motioned to the undercover to get in the garage and hide. So, get this, we couldn't get

Ramirez to deal with someone outside his own group, yet he took in some stranger just to fuck with the cops.

Well, as it turned out we used that 'stranger' to get multiple buys from Ramirez. We were into him good, but Terry was still unhappy with the way his CI was being used by Anthony and made it known loud and clear. "You're an asshole," he said to Anthony, as I got in the surveillance van. They were both arguing, which was no surprise since they hated each other. But we had work to do and this was not the time and definitely not the place.

"Fuck you, Terry," Anthony screamed back. "Frankie, get this motherfucker out of here before I kill him."

"Calm down, Anthony. What are you guys arguing about now?" I yelled at the both of them.

"This asshole cares very little about the health of my CI in this case," Terry said, pointing his finger at Anthony.

"Fuck you and your CI, Terry! He's just another fucking cock-sucking low life anyway." Anthony was really pouring it on and I could not figure out why he was so determined to be at odds with Terry. It pained me to say anything regarding this matter, but Terry was right and Anthony was wrong, period. Terry was just looking out for the safety of the CI and Anthony didn't get it.

THE BEGINNING

What Anthony did not understand, and quite frankly was not really paying attention to, was the age of this confidential informant. He was only eighteen. We rarely used people that young, for a variety of reasons and that was what Terry was trying to get across to Anthony, who was not hearing it.

I could not calm them down and Terry was still screaming at Anthony.

"He's just a kid, Anthony. He's gonna end up dead and you're using him the wrong way."

"Terry, let me explain this to you," Anthony stated, slowly. "This is a big case and it's affecting three jurisdictions and has ties to a much bigger target, who doesn't live on these streets. Instead, they're enjoying drinks in Columbia, while these kids are getting poisoned. So, I don't care what your concerns are here. I'm going to use your CI as I see fit, until blood runs out of his eye sockets if I have to, whether you like it or not. We'll hit this location next week. Then, you and your fucking fancy ways and your fancy clothes can take a walk, with your CI's feet hanging out of your fucking ass."

All Terry could do was just stare at Anthony. Robinson was a lot of things, but he wasn't stupid. The one thing Anthony was always good at was tipping his hand. It was a weakness of his, from when he was a kid, but it was also a bad habit to have in our business. This was not about the CI at all. This was about Agent Carter and the FBI. They had the bigger picture of this case and Anthony was going to be the one to

148

deliver it to them, no matter what. I now knew why Anthony was so interested in this case. I don't blame him for trying to better himself but you can't just disregard the safety of the people involved. Even if it is some low-life CI. The undercover's work was completed and even he was voicing concerns about how close the CI was to the target. He was in the house most of the time and he did not want the CI there for the arrest. The undercover had a feeling that Ramirez may have been onto the fact that someone was ratting on him. Remember, the CI was just a kid, he was not a trained narcotics agent like the undercover.

The day came to hit the house. Terry, myself, and Anthony were dressed in tactical gear. The SERT, Special Emergency Response Team, were to enter the house first and secure it and then we would follow them in.

As soon as the sun went down it was time. The search warrant had been secured for the house and was based on the buys we had made. We assembled the team and created a command post as far out of sight of any neighbors as we could. The SERT group were set up and ready, with a battering ram and flash grenades. It was time to end this group of drug pushing animals once and for all. Every dog has its day and no matter how smart you are, or how much control you think you exercise over your drug operation, it usually ends with you getting caught and doing time. Or you catch a bullet from us, or the competition, which signals the end of the line for good.

The SERT team was ready for war, with protective gear that left very few vulnerable areas where a stray bullet could find its mark. These guys loved what they did and were well-equipped as well, armed with MP5's, shotguns and they had snipers locked onto the windows and the front door of the premises. It was go-time and they were itching to move. I had tactical command over this investigation, which meant even if there was a higher ranked officer on the scene, I was in control. And in this case, no one was doing a thing until I gave them the go ahead.

"Come on, Frank," Anthony said. "Let's do it."

I wasn't hesitant and I got that everyone wanted to go. I just wanted to be careful. We were in a residential neighborhood, surrounded by a lot of innocent folks and I didn't want anyone to get hurt if I could help it. But I also knew we had to get this thing moving. I looked at Anthony, then the SERT team and gave them the go sign.

BAM! They smashed the door in using just one swing from the ram, and then you heard it. BOOM! The flash grenade went off and it must have hit a wall in the house because you could smell it burning after the blinding light dissipated. The team stormed the house and took Ramirez and one of his runners to the ground quickly. They couldn't see shit from the flash grenade, so it made it easy to take the guys down. In seconds, they were immobilized and cuffed. They didn't know what hit them.

With the location secure, the real work started and just like most shitheads we encountered, once they were caught they broke quickly, like little bitches, only concerned about themselves. They were ready to give up the next guy in line, to make a deal, hoping to avoid a cell for the next ten years.

Terry, Anthony, and I entered the garage and it looked like one of those warehouse nightclubs. The walls were all painted black and everything was staged perfectly. The only difference was that there was no bar and instead of strobe lights and speakers, the place was stacked floor to ceiling with stolen property. These guys had a little bit of everything. There were stolen phones, statues and Christmas gifts that were still gift wrapped. They even had a fucking iguana from a pet shop. The thing looked up at me from the tank and I couldn't believe it but it still had a price tag on one of its legs. The house was a gold mine, with loads of narcotics and paraphernalia used for packaging and distribution. There was plenty of weight in there to put these guys away for ten lifetimes. And while the drug haul was a great thing for the bust, what happened next was a heartbreaker. There was a loft located in the garage that had a ladder leading down to the main floor. We had to take a look as part of the search process, so I held the ladder while Terry went up to the loft. As Terry got closer he said he smelled something and it was not pretty.

I went up the ladder after Terry and smelled the odor, too. It was that kind of odor I had experienced more than a few times as a cop and knew that it was not going to be good. I found Terry standing over a crumpled mass that was partially concealed with a tarp. It was his CI. His head was bashed in; they had killed the kid. He hadn't been gone long, because rigor mortis had not yet set in.

Terry was just standing there, motionless, I looked at his face and it was all contorted, skewed into the ugliest expression I had ever seen. It was like a moment when something in his head must have snapped. All of sudden, he slumped to the ground, falling into a seated position. He put his head in his hands where it looked as though he wanted to sob, but nothing came out. Anthony came up behind us, completely unaware of the scene. He was so keyed up he didn't even take note of what had happened. He was oblivious to the presence of the kid, the smell, all of it. You see, when a person dies, their insides let go and as a cop, you usually know that smell. It's different from rotting. And Anthony missed it all.

"Hey, what else did you guys…?" Anthony started saying.

I stopped him with my hand on his chest and shushed him. Then Anthony saw the kid, and then he saw Terry, who was still slumped on the floor. I could see the anguish on Anthony's face. Terry looked up at Anthony and, at first, he did not say anything. He wasn't even angry. He just stared at Anthony and finally said, "Congratulations, you got your pound of flesh. You can go and tell his mother how he died, now." Then Terry just walked away. He was never the same after that night, never.

CHAPTER TWENTY-FOUR

Frank:

That bust came and went and the years seemed to whiz by after that, faster than I could have anticipated. I was getting closer to the magical twenty-year mark and retirement was looming. To be honest, even though I knew it was wrapping up, I found myself giving a whole new meaning to the term functioning alcoholic. My marriage was suffering, too and Mary and I were fighting all the time. This job was eating me up inside and my only escape seemed to come from the inside of a bottle.

"Mary, I have to work late tonight," I called to her as I was getting ready to leave.

"Save it, Frank," Mary said. "I know you'll be home late again, nothing new there."

"What do you want me to do?" I asked her, as I was tying my shoe.

"Say 'no.' That is what I want you to do. Say I can't work tonight, just because."

"Because… what?"

"How about, because my wife needs me. Your children need you. The boys need their father. I need my husband. How about that?"

"Mary, I'm sorry, I really am. I'm trying to balance it all. Between the side jobs, these heavy cases, I don't know what to do. Can't you be patient?"

"Frank, I have been patient and I'm not feeling right. I don't like what I'm feeling. I know your heart is in the right place for everyone, including your victims, your suspects, and your friends. Your family, though, Frank? Us! Frankie Jr. and Sal, they need you more than the rest of them."

"Mary, what do you want from me? I'm not abusive. I do what I can with the kids. This isn't a nine-to-five job, Mary. Everything is on my back. If I don't spend enough time with you and the kids, I'm a failure as a husband and a Dad? I don't put enough into my cases, I fail or get sued or worse, someone dies. I mean, there has to be some space for me."

"Oh, I think that you've found that space, Frank. You've found that space right inside a bottle and inside that bar that you think is more of a home than here. I'm not stupid. I see what's going on. You coming home blind drunk. I have a surprise for you, Frank. You may come home one night and find nothing but an empty house."

154

I needed to get to work and I'd had enough of Mary's crazy rantings. I knew deep down inside that she was right. I was losing it, but there was nothing I could do to stop it. It was like a runaway train and I could not find the brake. As I walked out the door, I looked back and it was beginning to all feel surreal to me. There were my children, my wife, and it was like they were out there in a twilight zone. The connection I once had was missing now and for a brief moment, I was scared. I didn't know what to do anymore. How could this happen? I loved my wife and children and fought not to make any mistakes at work, so I could come home to them. Yet, all of that didn't matter anymore, because in reality, it wasn't the job that was keeping me away from them. In some strange way, it was my love for them and the need to keep them safe that made me keep my distance.

That night came and went and sure enough, I found myself at Ron's Bar again. I was exhausted mentally. I was sipping a drink when I felt a hand on my shoulder and heard a familiar voice.

"Ron's? Why not the Saloon, like everyone else tonight?" Ricky Rosa asked.

I turned to see him and asked, "What's up, Boss?"

"Come on Frank, you know I hate when you call me that," Rosa responded, shaking his head.

"Well, that's what you are," I said, matter-of-factly.

"Really? Frank? You know better than that. Yeah, you work for me, but I am your friend first. Besides, you don't need me to tell you what to do. You could run this squad with your eyes closed."

"Then this is your lucky night, friend. You're in luck because according to Mary, my eyes are closed."

"Frank, you're a great detective and I've watched you over the years. You pour everything you've got into your job. You just don't want to make any mistakes and that effort consumes you."

"Mistakes?"

"Yes, mistakes," Rosa said, with a pause, too long of a pause for my liking.

"What the fuck are you trying to say, Ricky? That I'm obsessed? I'm fucked up? What is it?" I asked, defensively.

He put his hands up to try to calm me down. "Hey Frank, it's all right to make a mistake. In fact, it's healthy."

"Healthy?" I was wondering what he was leading up to. Was he talking about the job? Or my family?

"Yes, healthy," he replied shortly.

"Okay, genius. You have my attention, I'm listening."

"Frank, in your efforts to be perfect… and you are, hell, your cases are air-tight, you forgot what an error looks like."

"You mean, I didn't notice I was neglecting my family or the people around me? Is that what you're trying to say?"

"Something like that my friend. That is the error of your ways. That is the biggest mistake you are making and you don't even see it."

Ricky was right, as always, and all I could do was take a deep breath. "What can I do?" I asked, knowing what the answer was going to be and that it would be something that I couldn't do.

"Take some time off Frank. Spend it with your family. Get away from this job and all the demons that plague your mind. Take a breath of fresh air and then come back."

I looked at him, knowing he was right. "Maybe I will, Ricky, maybe I will."

Just then, my phone rang. It was headquarters. I answered my phone, not taking my eyes off Rosa, "This is Detective Risi, what can I do for you?

Dispatch answered. "We have a rape, Frank. She was found tied up on the side of the road, near the station. We don't need you at the scene. Just go straight to the hospital."

"Okay, no problem. I'll be right there."

Ricky looked at me and asked, "What do you got?"

"Rape victim. She was found tied up on the side of the road." I left a few dollars on the bar, downed what was left of my vodka before turning to Ricky. "Take some time off, huh? Just how do you think that happens? Here we go again, right back into the shit. My friend, there is no way to take time off."

As I hurried out of the bar I accidentally ran into a woman, causing her handbag to fall to the ground. I couldn't help but assist her in collecting the things that fell on the sidewalk. As we both stood up I locked eyes with her. I don't know what it was, but there was an instant connection with this woman.

"I'm sorry," I said, "I didn't mean to knock you over. I wasn't looking at where I was going."

Then a strange thing happened. She put her hand on my chest and it immediately brought a calming effect over me. "It's okay," she said, organizing her belongings. "But, you really should be more careful. You could run a girl over."

All I could do was keep apologizing and for some strange reason, I was at a loss for words.

"I'm sorry, I'm in a rush. Um… um… I didn't catch your name. You are…"

"Jackie, my name is Jackie Romano."

I then backed away from her and almost fell off the curb. "Nice to meet you, Jackie. I would love to stay and talk to you more, but I gotta go."

CHAPTER
TWENTY-FIVE

Frank:

I made it to the hospital, where I met with the rape victim, Nancy. I learned she was unconscious when they first brought her there. I also learned she didn't live in our city but instead lived in Terry's jurisdiction. So, I called dispatch and had them contact Terry's department to notify him to respond to the hospital. When I got to Nancy's room, she was alert and I was able to ask her some questions about what happened.

"Hello, Nancy. I'm Detective Frank Risi. First, let me say how sorry I am this happened to you. Do you think you're able to answer some questions for me?" I asked her as sincerely and sensitively as I could.

She nodded yes. I felt horrible for her. She had swelling and bruising to her face and bite marks all over her body. She was found in the street, discarded like a bag of garbage. She had rope burns around her wrists and ankles. A rape kit had been used to collect DNA for evidence, which, along with her cooperation, would be helpful. She had trouble speaking, but was willing to try.

"Nancy, I'm a little confused? You live a good distance away from here. Were you in this city, when you were hurt?" I asked.

160

"No, I wasn't," she replied. "He took me here and pushed me out of the car."

"He? Nancy, you know who did this to you?"

"What does it matter?" she cried out. "You're not gonna do anything to him, you can't."

"I can't? Who did this to you? Where did this happen?"

She was reluctant to answer. "Nancy, do you hear me?"

At that moment a uniformed officer entered the room, motioning that he needed to talk to me. A rape advocate stayed with Nancy while I left the room to see what the officer wanted. As I was walking out, it all hit me that once again, I was involved in another case that was going to be consuming. I was so fucking tired from drinking, yet I really wanted one. I was never prepared for this kind of case. They are so emotional and if you're not careful, or if you accidentally sound insensitive, you will have everyone against you. That was not a mistake I could afford to make.

"What do you want?" I said to the officer, annoyed that my questioning was interrupted.

"Detective Chris Hanna is at the crime scene where she was left, he wants you to contact him. Also, Detective Robinson is on his way here," the officer said.

"Hanna?" I asked. "Who the fuck is he?"

"He's our new Detective assigned to BCI."

"I don't want him, where is the Woodsman?"

"Sir, the Woodsman, I mean Detective Manning, just retired. He left the department last week."

"What? Last week? Why?"

"Well, Detective, he had an argument with Sergeant Rosa and told him to go fuck himself. He cleaned out his locker and now he's running around in the woods."

"The woods?"

"Yes, sir. In the woods. You know, he's making igloos and eating berries," the officer responded sarcastically.

"Fuck me. Okay, tell Hanna to process the scene and then have him come here ASAP to collect any evidence from the hospital personnel."

"Will do, sir."

As the officer left to go and contact Hanna, Terry Robinson had found his way to the hospital and we finally met up.

"What do you have Frank?" Terry asked.

I looked at Terry and could see that he still had that annoyed look, the same one he had ever since the drug bust with Anthony. I could see that Terry was living those moments in the garage over and over and that the effects of finding that dead kid laying there had never left him.

"I don't know, yet," I said to Terry. "It might not have even occurred in my jurisdiction."

"So why am I here?" Terry asked.

"She lives in your area. I thought you would want to be here from the start, in case it's yours."

"Whatever, let's go," Terry said, disgusted. He walked right into the room. I followed him and was going to let him take the lead on this for now.

"Nancy, this is Detective Terry Robinson."

"Hi, Terry," she said, as if she knew him and then started to cry.

Terry sat next to Nancy and asked, "Nancy, what happened to you?"

I cut in, "You two know each other?"

Terry shushed me, "One second, Frank. Nancy, who did this to you?"

"I'm afraid to say," she replied.

"Nancy, please answer me," Terry pressed her.

"He said he would kill me."

"Who? I'm not gonna let anything happen to you. Tell me," said Terry.

Nancy hung her head and mumbled, "It was Turner."

Terry's eyes grew as he questioned Nancy, "Turner? The father or Junior?"

"Turner? Turner who?" I asked. I looked at Terry, a bit lost. "I have several questions for you, Terry, like what's going on here?"

Terry stood up to meet me and whispered in my ear, "I'll explain later. She's talking about Ambassador Turner."

In my head, I was thinking, Ambassador Turner? He's ancient. It makes no sense.

Terry turned towards Nancy one more time, "Are you sure it was the Ambassador?"

Nancy took a second and then shook her head, "No, it was his son," she replied.

I stood there in dumb amazement. I was really confused now. It was the Ambassador, then it was not, then it was his son. What was going on here? But Terry cleared things up a bit.

"Look Frank, the Ambassador has a son. He's known as Junior. That's who Nancy is talking about," Terry said.

After Nancy was left to the attending nurse, we both left the room and that gave me the chance to confront Terry about the bizarre scene that had just played out between him and Nancy.

"You wanna tell me what the fuck is going on here?" I asked. "A few minutes ago she was reluctant to tell me anything about herself or the assailant. Now, she was beaten and raped by Ambassador Turner's son?"

"Frank, Nancy is a stripper. That's why she was reluctant to tell you anything. James Turner III loves to frequent strip joints. We call him Junior and he hates that," Terry explained. "He would drink too much, maybe cause a ruckus, but we never knew him to do anything like this."

"I never really heard much about him at all," I told Terry.

"Stop drinking Frank and get your head out of the sand. Read a newspaper every now and then and you might be up on current events. Look, I'll take this over from here. It probably occurred in my jurisdiction anyway," Terry said.

"How do you know it was in your jurisdiction? You know what, regardless of what you do, I wanna be there when you pick him up. Just in case it's mine."

"Fine," said Terry. "You fucking doubting me now, Frank?"

"Terry, go fuck yourself. Let's go back in and find out where this happened. Worse comes to worse you can have your forensics detective pick up whatever Hanna finds."

"Hanna, who the fuck is Hanna?" Terry asked. "What happened to Manning?"

"It's a long story, and if you picked up and read a newspaper every once in a while you would be up on current events, too, Terry."

I had enough of sparring with Terry and we both went back into Nancy's room to try and straighten this thing out. Dealing with Terry had become very difficult and I needed to get out of there. As it was, his thought process was all over the place. Once we got her talking, Nancy explained that she went out with Turner, but not for business. She had gone back to his apartment afterward which, by the way, was in Terry's jurisdiction. Then she wanted to leave. Well, that didn't happen and he had his way with her. Turner forced himself on her, becoming more violent as she rejected him. So in the process not only did she get raped, but she got her ass kicked as well.

It became clear that Robinson had his hands full with this case. James Turner III was indeed the son of James Turner, the U.S. Ambassador to Germany. He was a career politician, a staple in New York and well-known as a foreign-service officer. He was outspoken in the media and had a lot of connections in high places. The guy was hooked straight to the President of the United States.

166

Terry was right, though, I didn't know everything about him and his son. Who would? What the fuck did I care about their status in the world? I was sorry Nancy was raped and beaten and that, in and of itself, was enough to go and lock up that jackass Turner and throw away the key. The thing that bothered me more than just the crime was why did Junior dump Nancy's body in my jurisdiction? It was weird, given the circumstances. Maybe it meant nothing. Maybe, he just wanted to take her as far away from his house as possible? That would make sense. Rape her, beat her and then dump her far away.

The next day, I met with Detective Chris Hanna. This guy was a piece of work. He was a kid basically, a computer whiz who some say was too smart to be a cop. Apparently, his brain was like a hard drive. He had tons of shit stored in there, just waiting to spill out when asked the right question.

The guys nicknamed Hanna, "Short Circuit." You would think it was because of his skills, but as it turned out it was because he had one hell of a temper. He acted like everyone was bothering him, always annoyed at people, like they were not smart enough to be talking to him. I wasn't sure what I was going to get, but, with Manning's retirement, he was all I had.

"Hanna, good morning, I'm Frank Risi," I said, trying to get on his good side.

"What's so fucking good about it, Frank?" I just stared at him, thinking, there it was that famous short-circuit temper I'd heard about. I really wanted to stab him right there and then. But I needed this prick, so I had to go easy.

"Look, Hanna, I really don't give a shit about the day. All I want from you is whatever evidence you discovered last night where the rape victim was found. What I need you to do is please contact Detective Ferrara, who handles forensics for Terry Robinson, and update him on it. Whatever they want, just make it happen."

"Yeah, yeah, okay, I hear you, Risi. You don't have to break my balls. I'll get it done when I have time," Hanna said, not even looking up from his phone.

"No, you'll get it done now," I demanded.

Hanna, whose feet were on the top of his desk like he owned the place, didn't even blink as I screamed at him. He finally got up from the desk and as he was walking away, I could hear him mumbling to himself. All I could do was just shake my head before leaving the office. I kept wondering, "Where do they find these people?"

CHAPTER
TWENTY-SIX

Tommy:

My cousin Frank was in the bar early, earlier than usual, so I knew something was bothering him.

"Okay cousin, what is it?" I asked.

"How do you know something is bothering me, Tommy? I could just be visiting, ya know?"

"That's okay too, Frank. But let's be honest, you don't just visit, at least not at this early hour, unless there's something on your mind." I then leaned over and whispered in Frank's ear, *"Ti conosco meglio di te."*

When we were growing up, Frank and I made sure that we picked up the Italian language from our parents. We very rarely used it as we got older, except when we didn't want other people to know what we were saying, or when I wanted to make a point with Frank. And today I was making a point.

Frank finally found his tongue and responded, *"Immagino che tu lo faccia."*

Simply put, I was letting Frank know that I knew him better than he knew himself. Of course, he had to respond like a smart ass, telling me, "I guess you do." Frank was like that, he gave it just as good as he got it. Anyway, I continued to press him about what was wrong, because clearly there was something bothering him. "Well, you are here a little early in the day for starters. The other thing, you're holding onto an empty glass like it's the last one in the bar."

"That's unusual?" Frank replied.

"For you, it is," I joked.

"That's not funny, Tommy."

"I'm working on my comedic side, and this morning it looks like you could use a little cheering up." I grabbed Frank by the shoulders, trying to get him to relax a little.

For all my efforts, I could not get Frank to respond. He was just staring into space, oblivious to what was going on. Then he started talking, but not directly to me. It was like he was talking to the wall, still staring straight ahead.

"We had a bad rape a few days ago. You know I hate those things. They're very personal and the details always turn out to be too much for me to stomach."

"You did?" I interrupted. "Who was it?"

But instead of answering me right away, Frank played with his glass. I was a little worried about him just then. Frank had been a cop for a long time and very little rattled him. But he was rattled now and acting a little sketchy, too.

"Her name isn't important. And it's really not my case anyway. It's actually Terry's."

"So that's a news flash, another Terry Robinson gem? But you've had rapes before, so I'm not following you on this one."

"Tommy, you ever hear the name, James Turner?"

"Do you mean, the ambassador, or Jimmy, his kid? Yeah, I've heard of them. What of it?"

"Well, I mean Junior and he's hardly a kid and how the fuck does everyone know about him better than me? He's apparently a sicko and I never even heard of him."

"Well, Frank, if you read a newspaper every now..."

Right then and there Frank cuts me off. "Okay, I get it. I've heard this line before. I must have had my head in the sand when this guy emerged from the desert."

"Wow, we're touchy, Frank, aren't we? For the record, Turner frequents my establishments. He always comes in at night and sometimes he wears a wig to cover up that white fucking hair that stands out wildly on his head."

"Wait, he comes here? When did that start and how come you never told me anything about this?"

"Frank, I just told you."

"Look, Tommy, what does he come here for? No offense, but this is not the kind of joint an Ambassador's kid is known to hang out in."

"Not just here, Frank. He comes to both of my bars. He partakes in the pleasures of the ladies if you know what I mean. He's really a freak, but acts respectably and obeys my rules."

I could see that Frank was getting upset and the more I told him about this guy Turner, the more uptight he was becoming.

"Frank, what's eating you? Is it Turner being a freak or the fact that he's the Ambassador's kid? Or maybe both? Something's wrong, what is it?"

"Tommy, maybe it's nothing, but this guy was just accused of rape. And not just any rape, but a nasty, brutal one. The odd thing about it is..."

Frank just trailed off without saying anything else. It was as if he did not want to finish the sentence and that concerned me a little.

"The odd part is what, Frank?" Now I wanted to know what he was going to say.

"Never mind Tommy, I'll talk to you about this another time. I just need to wrap my head around this a little more before I say anything else."

"Okay! Have it your way," I replied, frustrated.

"Oh Tommy, there's one more thing. Who's this girl Jackie?"

"You mean Tina's sister?" Tommy asked.

"I guess," I answered.

"That's Tina Romano's sister. Jackie works for me as a stripper. Why are you asking, Frank? Has she done something?"

"No, no reason, I left here in a hurry the other night and almost ran her over."

"Did you apologize?"

"Um, yeah, of course. I got to go. See you later."

"Okay, see ya, Frankie." I just shook my head. What the fuck was bothering him now? Jackie was a good girl, so what could she have done to get Frank interested in her?

CHAPTER TWENTY-SEVEN

Frank:

While Nancy was recovering from her injuries, Terry picked up Turner and brought him to his headquarters for the purpose of interviewing him regarding the rape. Terry knew that he had to tread carefully with Turner because of how well-connected he was. He contacted me prior to picking him up, so I met him in his Detective Division just after he had returned and he had Turner waiting in the interview room.

"Frankie, I have Turner, he's in the office," Terry said.

"Does he know why he's here?" I asked.

"I just told him I wanted to speak with him regarding a matter and he came voluntarily."

"Hmm, wow!" I said, completely surprised at how willing Turner was to come in.

"Okay Terry, I'll sit in while you speak with him."

As we were walking to the interview room, an officer called to Terry. He was holding a phone and covering the receiver.

174

"Detective, you have a phone call," the officer said.

"Who is it? What do they want?" asked Terry.

"It's Paige Brown. A reporter. She says she's coming here and wants to speak with you regarding your rape case."

Terry looked at me like it was my fault. I put my hands out, gesturing that I had no idea what was going on, despite the fact that I knew Paige was a nosy journalist who seemed to find out more than she should.

"She's your friend, too," I said to Terry. "What did you expect? You know Paige gets around and she probably heard all about this. And since Turner is involved, this could be a big story for her."

Terry said to the officer, "When she gets here, tell her I'm busy and I'll speak to her later. And do not let her near us."

As we both continued to the interview room, I felt like everything was moving in slow motion. Terry opened the door and sitting there was James Turner. I had never seen him in person, so I took a long hard look. Turner was forty-seven years old and while he was a sizable man, he wasn't heavy. I noticed that he had a reddish hue to his face, like a man who spent a lot of time in bars, consuming a great deal of alcohol. I hate to say it, but having put in my fair share of time in the bar, it was easy to spot a habitual drinker. He had a thick, bushy head of hair and it was all white, shocking white, the kind that stands out and could not be missed in a crowd. It was half styled and half messed up, almost like he kept it that way on purpose. He was taking in his surroundings, marveling at everything like they were new toys that he wanted to play with.

"Jimmy Turner, I'm Detective Terry Robinson. And this is…"

Turner put his hand up, stopping Terry in mid-sentence. "Well, it is about time," he blurted out. "Finally, I am graced with the presence of the great Detective Frank Risi. I've been waiting to meet you for a long time, Detective."

I stared at him for a second. There was a lot going on here and it wasn't good. I replied, trying to contain my puzzlement, "I'm not so sure how to take that, Mr. Turner. You seem to have me at a disadvantage. You know me, but I don't believe I've ever had the opportunity to make your acquaintance."

Terry looked at both of us unsure whether to interrupt or not. If Turner was gonna show his hand, any trained detective would certainly have let this play out.

"I have so much admiration for you, Frank," said Turner.

I chuckled at that. "Well, I'm glad I could keep you entertained, Mr. Turner."

"No Frank, you don't entertain me. You intrigue me. You see there is a difference."

176

This guy was creepy and I really did not like interviewing people like that. First of all, they are hard to read and second, even more difficult to predict.

Terry was losing his patience with what was starting to look like a game between Turner and me. Just as he was ready to put an end to this meaningless banter, Turner stopped him once again.

"How can I help you guys?" Turner asked as he slapped his hands together, before vigorously rubbing them.

Terry looked at him incredulously and said, "Junior, I…"

Again, Turner stopped him and in a voice mimicking a Shakespearean actor said, "Oh no, no, that won't do, at all. I despise the name Junior, Terry. You will address me properly, or not at all."

Terry gave him that look. I had seen it before. It was 'The I wanna smack the shit out of you' look. "Mr. Turner," Terry said.

Again Turner stopped him, this time I could see that Terry was getting visibly upset and in danger of losing his temper.

"Jimmy will do, Terry," said Turner.

And as I suspected would happen, Terry lost it, telling Turner, "And you can lose the Terry shit, right now, okay? It is Detective or Detective Robinson. Got it, Turner?"

"Testy aren't we?" Turner replied. "Okay, have it your way. You may proceed, Detective."

Terry sighed. Yup, Turner had succeeded in getting under his skin. Point of fact, it was not hard to get to Terry these days. He had developed a soft underbelly and was vulnerable to any kind of attack. And unfortunately, in the harsh world we lived in, that was a very bad position for a detective to be in. However, regardless of how he felt, I had to give Terry credit for pressing on with the interview.

"Jimmy, where were you two nights ago?" Terry asked.

"Hmmm... two nights ago?"

"Yes," said Terry.

Turner just looked at him for a moment, as though he were contemplating an answer. He rubbed his chin and rubbing his hands together, took a few deep breaths. "Well, it was the evening, right?" Turner asked.

"Yes," said Terry.

"I would have eaten dinner for sure. I think I had a date."

"A date?" I said. "Who would that be with, Jimmy?"

"Hmmm, I'm not too sure of her name. I think it rhymes with rancy or rancid, yes, maybe she was rancid." All of sudden Turner broke out into laughter as if he was amused by some private joke. But, as quickly as he'd begun laughing, he became deadly serious again, leaning in and adding, "What did that bitch say?"

"Bitch?" Terry asked. "Is that what she is? A bitch? Or is there more Turner?"

I could see Terry was trying to get to Turner and for obvious reasons. Some detectives would have thought that this line of questioning would lead to an easy admission. I knew that Turner was just fucking with us and everything going forward was going to be tied to a riddle. This was damn peculiar at best. Why would a guy like Turner, with the connections his father had, just voluntarily come to a police station without representation? Then be subjected to an interrogation about a woman he had beaten and raped and of whom he referred to as a bitch. Who does that? This guy was definitely twisted, but there was more to it than that, because he was having fun with us and clearly had no fear of being locked up.

As Terry began to ask him another question, the expected happened next; through the door marched half the population of one of those high priced downtown law firms. They came, of course, with their standard proclamation: "Detectives, we're assigned to represent James Turner. He will not be making any statements. Is he under arrest?"

THE BEGINNING

Terry looked at me like somebody had just come in and pulled the rug out from under his feet. Turner's lawyers had interrupted the lovely show he was putting on for us.

"Detectives," the lawyer said again, "Is Mr. Turner under arrest?"

Terry looked at me and then glanced at everyone in the room. "No, he is free to go. For now."

"Thank you, Detectives. Come, Jimmy," the lawyer said.

It was like he was talking to a child as Turner obediently got up from the table to leave the room. As they started walking out to the main hallway, we both followed them. I could hear the lawyer saying to him, "How many times have I told you never to speak to the police without calling us first?"

Turner looked back at me, saying, "But they are *so* interesting."

As we got to the lobby, who the fuck was there? It was none other than Paige Brown.

"Detectives, any comments on why Ambassador Turner's son is in custody?" Paige asked.

"Paige, no one is in custody," said Terry.

She just ignored Terry and kept trying to push her way past us to get to Turner.

180

"Detective Risi, any comments?" she asked, sticking her microphone in my face.

The lawyer just looked at Paige scornfully. "There is no story here and no one is under arrest. Isn't that correct, Detectives?"

Before any of us could answer, Turner stopped and looked at all three of us and said, "Paige Brown! I just love your writing style."

"Well, thank you, Jimmy," as only Paige could answer. She was a girl who never shied away from a compliment. She did not even realize it was coming from a madman.

I was thinking at this point, what the fuck? Then, as Turner and the lawyers walked away, he turned around again and, looking at us, smiled, saying, "I'm so glad I was able to bring us all together."

One of the lawyers grabbed him by the shoulders and pushed him out the door, saying, "Will you shut the fuck up for Christ's sakes."

Once they were out the door, I needed to vent my confusion to Terry. "Terry, why did you let him go? Nancy identified him and it was an open and shut case. He did it and was about to gloat about it until his army of lawyers showed up."

"Frank, I spoke with Nancy and she's not going to cooperate. And you know what that means. No complainant – no arrest."

"What the…? Are you kidding me? Why did we bother to bring Turner in at all if you knew you had no complainant? What was that, an exercise in futility, or did you enjoy being humiliated by that freak?"

"Oh stop it, Frank. You heard me. Nancy doesn't want to cooperate, that doesn't mean there isn't value in interviewing Turner. A guy like that, this was not the first time he did something like this. What about your forensics? Did they find anything with the rape kit?"

"It was all negative," I said. "It wouldn't matter anyway. At best we can only confirm it was a date. No DNA. No fingerprints, nothing. It was like that fuck wasn't even there."

Terry had a point and I walked away more puzzled than when I'd gotten there.

I went back to headquarters where I ran into Anthony.

"What the fuck were you doing with Flash?" Anthony asked me.

"Rape case, involving James Turner and why can't you just get over this thing with Robinson? You don't need to keep insulting him with that fucking Flash nickname. That's why he doesn't like you."

"Fuck him. He is a piece of shit and I am never gonna be friends with him. He's a hot dog and only cares about himself. I need to look out for me."

"You know this guy Turner, Anthony?"

"Not through the job, Frankie."

"What do you mean?"

"Well, let's just say Carter is not the only one that frequents Tommy's clubs. Turner loves the strip clubs and why he's a freak, is because he sometimes comes there in disguise. He comes in wearing these wacky wigs like no one is going to recognize him. And he likes the girls a lot, if you get my meaning."

I should have known that Anthony would have been up on what happened in Tommy's bars. As it was, he was more involved with Tommy these days than ever, which I thought was a *big* mistake on his part. He wanted to join the FBI and there he was doing whatever he was doing for my cousin and make, no mistake, I knew it was not even close to being legal. But, Anthony liked to take risks and he liked the extra cash that came along with doing little errands for Tommy.

It was obvious Anthony would know who came and went more than I ever would. Just as well. I didn't want to know about any of that shit, even though Tommy never gave up on trying to suck me into his world. It was bad enough that I drink at his places.

I told Anthony that Turner walked away clean on this one. Nancy got scared for whatever reason and backed away from taking this guy down. I told him all about the army of lawyers that showed up and his little scene with Paige. It was all a shit show and nothing came out of it.

"I keep telling you, Frankie, that things are not always as they seem," Anthony said. "I know this guy Turner. He is hooked up to his ears, so having a team of lawyers show up to spring him should be of no surprise. I told you this guy is nuts and a complete weirdo."

I could see that Anthony was right. Every once in a while he was spot on the mark. And to tell you the truth, I was spooked over the way it happened, with Nancy being dumped in my jurisdiction. Was it deliberate and if so, why? The other thing that kept gnawing at me had to do with this guy's infatuation with me. What was all that great Detective Risi shit all about?

CHAPTER TWENTY-EIGHT

Frank:

When I came home that night I found a note on the kitchen table instead of dinner. The note was from Mary and I had a sinking feeling in the pit of my stomach that I knew what it was going to say. She had taken off and had no plans of coming back. The letter said all the things I expected. Better than that, it said all the things I was doing and not doing, to sustain the marriage and the relationship with the kids.

"Dear Frank,

I am sure that this letter is not going to come as a shock to you, but I have done everything in my power to get you to see that you have a wife and a family and that they should come first in your life. You say that I don't understand; that you need to make a living, do well at your job and keep us safe. I believe you. But I look at where we are and ask myself at what cost does all this happen? I could do with less money in exchange for more time with you.

And there are other things too, Frank. I am not blind. The drinking is completely out of control. You live at Tommy's bars, and I have seen the girls that rub up against you, trying to get your attention. I am not stupid Frank. You exist in a world that the kids and I could never be a part of. For all the efforts you have made

185

not to become like Tommy, you have failed. You are just like Tommy. The only difference between you and him is that you wear a badge and belong to a different gang.

My mind is made up and divorce is the only answer now. I just can't live with the person you have become.

- Mary."

I just stood there, frozen, as the reality of what had happened to me sunk in. That was it and Mary was right. Had I really become just like Tommy?

Everything was so eerie at that moment. The house was dead quiet, the bedrooms had some half-filled cardboard boxes and the dresser drawers in all the rooms were almost empty. It was as if no one had lived there at all. I couldn't help but think of the family as I walked by the pictures still hanging in the living room. My life was encapsulated in a snapshot, one picture after the other, year after year, and now it was as if it had never happened. A chapter of my life erased, and all I was left with was the thought of what do I do now?

* * *

My drinking had taken on a whole new level since Mary and the kids moved out. She wanted nothing to do with the house. She said it had too many memories. I agreed. I wasn't one of those people that could live in a house that wasn't a home anymore. So I sold it. We didn't have much equity in it, just enough to break even. Mary did not even fight me over the money. She just wanted me to take care of the kids. That was all.

With the house gone, I became an apartment dweller. It was a cold, solitary existence, where I felt as if my soul had evaporated. I was alone for the first time in my life, truly alone. I had no wife, no family, no real friends, just the police department. Did it really all come down to that? Was my identity limited to being just Detective Frank Risi?

It was a rough patch for me. My life was limited to a few personal possessions that were still tucked away in moving boxes. Anytime I would open them, I would cry in a corner of the room. There was just no one there that could ease my pain. Mary was done with me. I lost her, my home, my children, and my security. Not to mention the debt. There was child support for two kids and since Mary never worked, I had to give her alimony, never mind that she was going to get a piece of my pension, too. I had no idea where I was going to get all that money to pay her. I was sick of working second jobs, all those hours wasted at security gigs. It was blood money and in the end, it didn't help anyway.

You see, when you go through a divorce, the pain is not just about the separation itself. It's about all the things that ever happened to you in your life and all the things you didn't do right.

I kept reliving those last moments with my family. I think I did it in an effort to hold onto what I once had with them. I was angry with her, but also remember vividly the one final private moment we had together, one she would probably never admit happened where she was crying, telling me she was losing her best friend. But her mind was made up, and you never really know it's over until the papers are signed and those shithead lawyers get their payday. And then just like that, I lost my best friend, my first love, and there was no going back.

*   *   *

Mary:

Let's face it, everyone gets to that point in their marriage where things kind of fizzle out, right? I couldn't be the only one who wasn't in love with my husband anymore. My friends all complained about their marriages. Susan's husband controlled every move she made and every dollar she spent. Kristy's husband didn't pay her any mind and they lived more like roommates than husband and wife. With Frank and I, it felt like I wasn't even a priority. It was always about work, a case he had or who he was trying to impress. And if it wasn't about work, it was about the kids. It was like he was using all of that as an excuse to not be a part of our relationship. And let's not forget that he was spending more and more of his free time at Tommy's bars. Any wife would be uncomfortable with their husband being around strippers all the time like that. But, I was supposed to be okay with it since he was conducting "business" while he was there. Honestly, I was getting sick and tired of it. And the more I expressed my frustration, the more Frank seemed to distance himself from me. I couldn't find a happy medium.

I did, however, find a distraction. And while I'm not proud of it, I did what I had to do to maintain my sanity. At the deli I went to every week, there was a guy that worked there named Jack. He was a little younger than me and always treated me with respect, calling me "Mrs. Risi," in such a way that I felt like royalty. One afternoon, he was manning the store by himself and I was the only customer. As he was filling my order, he talked to me and I genuinely enjoyed his conversation. After he was done, he handed me my change and let his hand slip over mine. I just froze and looked into his eyes. He knew what I was thinking and I knew what he was thinking. He asked for my number, asked if we could talk again. I knew I shouldn't have even entertained the thought, but I was desperate for the attention and desperate for the conversation. I instead asked for his number and told him I would call him. I couldn't have him calling the house and all.

That was four months ago and I've talked to Jack almost every day since, sometimes for hours while the kids were at school. It was amazing to feel so alive while talking to someone, but it also drew attention to how incredibly distant Frank and I had become. He and I should have talked like that, not me and some stranger. One day I opened up to Susan about Jack and she lit into me. She asked me why I was even with Frank if I couldn't talk to him. She said Frank had lost me a long time ago and I should leave him while I still had my looks and youth. I knew she was right but was afraid to break up my family and was scared to be alone.

Finally, one day, Frank came home from work. I was sitting at the kitchen table, reading the paper. He walked right by me like I didn't exist. Not even a "hello" or a kiss on the cheek, nothing. I'd never felt so utterly alone. One of the worst feelings is to be in a relationship and still feel alone, but that's how it ended up with Frank. The saddest thing about it was that he didn't even realize what was going on. He always thought he was doing everything he should, but never reached far enough across the table to meet me. That day, possibly even that one moment, was the impetus that drove me to make the decision to leave Frank. While he didn't deserve to lose his marriage, I didn't deserve to sit around idle while he acted like everything was okay.

*   *   *

Tommy:

My cousin was devastated and he was drinking heavily. I always felt like he didn't do enough things wrong to end up like he did. There were the legal battles and the fact that his children chose her side. It all made him bitter. He would never know this, but his life and the way it fell apart were the reason why I never had a wife or a family. Why bother, if all they were going to do is abandon you anyway? Frank, to me, was a good husband and a great father. Yet his life just fell apart and I was now watching him self-destruct.

Frank was at the bar one night, lamenting into a glass of Tito's. "Tommy, how could I have done any better? Do you think if I had quit, Mary would have stayed around?"

That was Frank's life, always thinking about what he should have done differently while crawling deeper and deeper into the bottle.

"Frank, don't you think you've had enough to drink?" I asked him. "You've been here every night for weeks now. You need to get over this and start to put your life back together. Enough is enough."

"I know," Frank replied, as he continued to sip away at the endless stream of vodka.

*   *   *

Frank:

So I'm at the bar one late afternoon, my head buried in the newspaper (yes, I was actually reading the paper those days), nursing a glass of Tito's and seltzer when one of the girls came over and tried to seduce me with a lap dance. I thought they all knew better, so without looking up I tried to wave her off. I got annoyed with her when she wouldn't go away. Then I looked up from the paper and recognized the face. It was Jackie. I have no idea what hit me, or where my head was at, but I was awestruck. I mean she was beautiful.

I remembered our last encounter. It was on the street after I had nearly knocked her over. It was her touch that came back to me most poignantly. It was a slight caress of her hand and instantly I was calm. I was also at a loss for words at the time but knew I would have loved to meet her again.

Jackie was about thirteen years younger than me. She had dark hair, warm eyes, and an olive-skinned body that was just off the charts. She was of an Italian and Spanish mix, which gave her a flair and exoticness that was incomparable. She spoke Spanish fluently, but in a way that was animating to watch. I saw her tell off a few people in Spanish, the hands flying and those eyes all aglow, hair being tossed here and there. Jackie was a sight to behold. She had something that made me want to be around her, whether she spoke or not. And tonight she was speaking to me.

"It's Frank, right?" asked Jackie as she continued to dance around me.

"Yes, it is. I see you remembered." I was flattered.

"Why? Would you think I wouldn't?"

"I mean, I only ran into to you for a second. I know for me, it would be hard to forget you and that smile of yours."

"That's true," said Jackie, giggling. "And flattery will get you everywhere Frank."

She sat next to me, calling Trish, the bartender over. "One wine for me Trish, and a vodka, I think it is, for this lonely guy sitting next to me. It's on me," Jackie said.

I looked around for my cousin. I did not want to get Jackie jammed up. I realized she was a working girl and for Tommy, no less. I'd never talked to any of the girls that worked for him before. Hell, I kinda thought none of his girls were allowed to speak to me, let alone buy me a drink. But I could see that Jackie did not care and if Tommy got a little pissed, I would smooth it over.

We talked for hours and a few guys were coming over to Jackie to get her to dance. What could I say, she was working. When she refused, one of them started becoming irate. Then out of nowhere my cousin just grabbed the guy's shoulder and showed him through the door. At first, I was waiting for Tommy to let me have it for occupying so much of Jackie's time. But then he came over and I could see that he did not have that Tommy scowl that stopped people dead in their tracks.

"Jackie, I see you met my cousin Frank."

"Your cousin?" Jackie said, somewhat startled. She then started to apologize. "I'm sorry, Tommy, I didn't know."

Tommy put his hand up, signaling for Jackie to stop apologizing and said, "You're done working tonight. Why don't you keep Frankie company? Besides, I haven't seen him laugh this much in a long time."

"Thanks, Tommy," Jackie said. "I need the money, though. I'll finish my shift and then we can hang out."

"No need, I will pay you anyway. Go get dressed. I'll keep your seat warm until you get back."

Jackie jumped up and hugged Tommy in excitement. Then she looked at me and said, "Don't you leave me, because I will find you."

I couldn't stop laughing. I don't think she knew I was stuck to that seat and wasn't going anywhere.

"You like her, Frank?" Tommy asked.

I nodded my head and said, "Yes I do."

"Well, I don't normally give my girls up to anyone. But I think I can make an exception for my down and out cousin," Tommy said, snickering.

"You're an asshole, Tommy."

Tommy just laughed and gave it back to me, "Yeah but you love me anyway."

Just as the banter between Tommy and I came to an end, something surreal happened. Yes, I had been drinking, but my senses were still sharp as a tack. Out of the corner of my eye, I noticed a man coming closer and closer to me. I hated carrying my gun in a bar, most cops do, but for me, I saw it as a catastrophe waiting to happen. You always think you will get too fucked up and use it prematurely and that was a sure fire way to jackpot off the job. But this was different because I recognized this guy and wished I had my gun right then and there.

"Hello, Frank and Mr. DePriati. Isn't she pretty?"

It was Jimmy Turner.

"What?" I said.

"Your girl, Jackie. I think she's pretty."

Turner looked at the ceiling when he spoke and repeated himself.

"She's pretty. And, she's new, right Tommy?"

Tommy just looked at him, not sure where he was coming from. "Ah, Jimmy, why don't you get the fuck away from us?" Tommy said, trying to keep his composure.

"Excuse me," Turner replied. "I was not trying to piss you off and I didn't mean to interrupt. See, I had just recently spent some time with your cousin and I thought it would be rude to not at least say hello."

All I could do was stare at Turner. I was thinking, he was watching me and Jackie all that time. What a creep. "Well, Junior, you've had your fun. Now take a walk," I instructed. And since I knew calling him Junior was going to get to him, I waited for the rage to come. I wanted him to do something stupid. Sure enough, Turner developed that twisted look on his face, almost as if someone had just stabbed him with a needle.

"Now, Frank, friends don't talk to each other like that," said Turner and then raising his voice, he continued, "And Frank, we both know that you are better than that."

Tommy sensed what was going on and motioned over to Benny, giving the nod, as if saying, 'It's time for this prick to go.'

Turner was quick to pick up on Benny approaching and said suddenly, "Okay, I'm leaving. No need to touch me, Benny. My apologies to all of you."

Jackie walked over just as Turner was leaving. As he passed Jackie, Turner turned to her and said something. Jackie made a face and then shrugged it off.

"What did he say to you?" I asked.

"He told me to be nice to you," Jackie answered.

Tommy stood up. "Right, excuse me, you two have a good time together," and left the bar. Benny nodded at me and left, also. I guess the party was over, or at least the show was, anyway. And despite how weird that whole thing with Turner had been, I was just happy to be around Jackie.

"Do you want to get something to eat?" I asked Jackie, hoping to extend our time together.

"Okay. I'm definitely hungry. I could eat a horse."

Surprisingly enough, so was I. Since my ordeal with Mary, I had lost so much weight. The divorce had taken a toll on me and I did not have the appetite for food. It felt good to actually feel hungry, to want to share a meal with someone, especially Jackie. I walked out with her and as I passed my cousin, I mouthed, "Thank you." He just tipped his drink and off we went.

CHAPTER TWENTY-NINE

Frank:

The time I spent with Jackie was incredible and we became inseparable. Even though we were together all the time, the physical part of our relationship progressed slowly. I did not want to mess this up and besides it had been a while since I was physical with a woman. Most people would think sex would have happened right away, especially since Jackie was a stripper and all. She wasn't like that, though. Jackie had morals and the stripping thing was just a way to make a living. It was not about blowing a guy or giving him a quickie in the bathroom stall. It was just a job.

Jackie lived with her sister, Tina, because their parents were both deceased. They only had each other. Tina worked in healthcare and in her free time, she worked with abandoned pets. She had a heart of gold, but like so many of us, Tina was alone. She wasn't much older than her sister, but she cared for her like a mother would a daughter. Yes, she did not approve of Jackie dancing as a stripper for a living, but she couldn't deny Jackie had a look and charming personality that just drew people to her naturally. And she was smart, using all her allure to make money without having to compromise herself.

198

ALLIANCE

I don't think Jackie planned on running into anybody at that point in her life, especially a drunk, divorced detective. When you do things for a living that set you outside the norms, outside of what people call the civilized world, there tends to be a like-minded attraction. Like a nurse or a cop and yes, even a stripper. For me and Jackie, it was like that. We were attracted to each other for no other reason than we lived in a world very few people understood. And it was working well for us.

Jackie had been coming to my apartment regularly and I was doing better financially. After dating a bit, the night had finally come for her and me to get together in a different way. Just like most nights, Jackie came over to hang out. I had been relaxing and was sitting in the living room reading the paper when she came in.

"Frank, are you hungry?" she asked.

"Yes, I'm starving."

"Okay, I'm gonna go change and then I'll make us some dinner."

"That sounds great, baby."

I heard the bedroom door shut and I poured myself a drink. I had cut down on the alcohol considerably and was no longer drinking to get lost in myself, but rather because I enjoyed the taste. That was something I had never done before meeting Jackie. I savored that first sip and felt that everything was right for a change.

Then the bedroom door opened and Jackie walked out with just a blanket around her. I had gone back to the couch and the newspaper to wait for her, not expecting anything to happen except dinner. But when I looked up, Jackie dropped the blanket, exposing the sexiest body I had ever seen. Her skin was silky smooth and she looked like a piece of art – a perfectly sculpted masterpiece waiting to be enjoyed.

She looked at me, smiling. "Well, Frank, you said you wanted something to eat. So dig in."

I stood up and she kissed me. She ripped my shirt open and started kissing my chest. I removed my clothing and she stepped back and looked at me. Then she pushed me down and straddled me, moving her hips slowly, in and out, until I couldn't take it anymore. Jackie was heaven on earth and I was about to enjoy all the fruits she had to offer. I picked her up and carried her into the bedroom. We were in there for a long time.

As we lay together afterward, we sipped some wine while we talked. "That was just as I thought it would be Frank," Jackie said. "Not bad for an old guy."

I laughed at her and responded. "Yup, and you were not half-bad yourself."

She looked at me and we both laughed. We were having that moment, a time where two hearts come together, where two minds are in sync. I knew that I could not waste another opportunity in my life to be happy.

So, I did it. I had to say it. I had to let Jackie know what I was feeling right then and there.

"Look, Jackie, I don't know what tomorrow will bring. Life is short and I don't want to waste any of it. I want you to know that I love you." There, I'd said it and then held my breath for what was to come.

She stared at me, at first, looking even a little dumbfounded. I was wondering if I had made a mistake. Saying 'I love you' are the three most difficult words to say to anyone, especially after you had lost everything. But then Jackie's eyes lit up and she found her voice.

"Well, Frank, I guess that makes me a lucky girl."

"It does? I mean... yeah, it does."

She looked me straight in the eyes and kissed me gently on the cheek. Drawing close to my ear, she whispered, "And you are lucky as well because I love you too."

CHAPTER THIRTY

Tommy:

With Jackie shacking up with my cousin, Frank was the happiest I had seen him in a long time. I decided to have a little party at Ron's, a private one, just for a few of my close friends and family. I invited Jackie and Frank. Tina, Paige, and Anthony were there, along with Flatts, Scopa and a few other female "friends" too, if you get me.

"Frankie, I'm glad you guys could come," I said as I gave him a bear hug.

We were all bombed and having a great time, even Benny. And for Benny to let loose, you knew he was having a good time. You see, Benny was the kind of guy that always needed to be in control and for him to let his guard down, that meant a lot.

"Well, well, look at you two lovebirds," Anthony said to Frank and Jackie.

Frank responded, "Hey, Anthony, what's up?"

"You tell me, Frankie," he replied.

"I rarely see you these days. You must be working hard at the job."

"Yeah, Frank, they're driving us crazy down there. Then again, you've been kind of invisible lately, so I guess you wouldn't know."

I saw that Frank and Anthony were bullshitting a bit, which was nice to see. It's rare lately that we get together like this. It hit me that Anthony didn't even know that Jackie and Frank were a thing now. So I nudged Frank, kinda letting him know that he should explain his situation to Anthony.

"Shit, I just realized, you guys have never met," Frank blurted out. "This is Jackie. Jackie Romano. Jackie, this is Anthony."

"Nice to meet you, Anthony," Jackie said, as she shook his hand.

"I had heard that you found someone and are settling down again. Now I see what you've been doing lately and why you haven't been around," Anthony replied. "Can't say I blame you." He tipped his drink to Frank, "*Salute,* Frankie. And you as well, Jackie."

Anthony whispered into Frank's ear, "She's beautiful, my friend."

"Thanks," Frank replied. "So, what are you up to these days?"

"You know, just working and getting closer to leaving," Anthony said.

"I'm kinda surprised you're still here to be honest," Frank said.

"Well, Rome wasn't built in a day, Frankie," Anthony stood up to leave. "Nice to meet you, Jackie."

The party was coming to an end and I was talking to Tina, "You must be happy for your sister, right?"

Tina kind of scowled at me, "Happy, Tommy? Oh, for Frank being with her? Yeah. As soon as Jackie's out of here and away from all this shit, I'll be shooting confetti in the air."

I could see that Tina was not happy with me. It was not my fault that Jackie worked at my club as a stripper. She needed money. She was a looker, so who was I not to give her a job. But I knew there was more because I could see that look in Tina's eyes that screamed, 'I hate you, for Samantha being gone.' And I was not going to let her get away with her contempt for me. After all, I was just trying to help.

"Confetti, huh?" I snickered at Tina. "I don't pay her with confetti, so I'd watch your comments, Tina."

"Or what, Tommy?" Tina said, coming within inches of my face, "I'll disappear like Samantha?"

We were standing eye to eye. Tina was one tough bitch and I had to admire her for acting the part, but I didn't know whether to kiss her or stab her. Then Paige came over, but I could see that Tina was still fuming. She then turned her sights on Paige.

"Finally out of the bathroom, I see. What's the matter, Paige? You seem to be walking funny," Tina scoffed.

That was cold of Tina because everybody knew what Paige was doing in the bathroom. It was like her private bedroom, where she and Jameson never failed to get it on.

"Go fuck yourself, Tina," Paige replied, grabbing a fresh drink from the bar. Tina started to move towards her and it was clear a cat-fight was about to escalate.

But, Scopa was on his game and he saw that the two of them were about to get into it. "Come on Tina, let me show you the back office," Scopa offered, as he took her arm and started to lead her away from Paige. "This is no place for a fight."

Paige yelled after them, "Yeah, take her to the back room and give it to her hard Scopa, maybe the bitch will loosen up a bit."

With that, Tina lunged towards Paige, but not before Scopa picked her up and dragged her off to the back room. What a night and it ended at just the right time, otherwise I might have had two bruised up girls and a nasty conclusion to what was really a fun affair.

CHAPTER THIRTY-ONE

Frank:

So with everything going great with Jackie, it was time for me to get on with my life and leave the misery of the past behind. I rented a house upstate, with some land. It had a great view and offered some privacy and peace for the two of us. Jackie moved in and we were making the place our own. She had been going to college and was working less for my cousin. She was no longer dancing, just bartending. Her plan was to go corporate and work in Human Resources.

One night the phone rang and woke us from a deep sleep.

I answered, "Hello?"

"Frank? It's Toro."

"Vinny?"

"Yeah."

"What did they give you, a break from narcotics, kid?" I asked him.

"I begged for one. Listen, Frank, never mind that. You need to get down here as quick as you can."

"Why? What's happened?"

"Another rape. This one was beaten badly, Frank. Looks like a dump job, too. They found her at the back of Ron's."

Toro was explaining things quickly but paused for a minute. "Frank, she had a note taped to her."

"What? I'm on my way." I turned to Jackie, gave her a kiss on the cheek and told her, "I have to run."

"Okay, honey, better you than me," she said with a slight smile.

I responded to Ron's bar first, since the victim had already been taken to the hospital and was in no condition to talk. As I walked into the rear parking lot, I was met by Sergeant Rosa and Detective Hanna.

"You wanna tell me what the fuck is going on?" said Rosa. I just ignored him.

I turned my attention towards Hanna. "Is this where she was found?" There was a lot of blood.

"Yeah, Frank," said Hanna. "She was beaten pretty good and had cigarette burn marks on her. Like whoever did this pressed hard to put them out."

"Frank, they left a note," said Hanna. "I bagged it."

"What did it say?"

"I bagged it," he repeated, annoyed. "I'll take it back to the office and put it in the tank and fume it for possible prints."

"What did it say, Chris?" I was getting pissed off that I had to keep repeating myself.

"It really doesn't matter," Hanna responded and tried turning away from me.

I grabbed him by the collar, yelling, "I won't ask you again."

"It said 'BOO,' Frank. It said 'BOO.' What the fuck did you do, Frank? Did you anger the boogie man?" asked Hanna.

I looked around and felt a chill down my spine as if someone was watching us.

"I'll contact Terry Robinson," I said.

"Why?" asked Hanna.

"Yeah, why Frank?" Rosa echoed.

I took a breath and exhaled. "Because it happened in his jurisdiction," I said, getting ready to leave.

"How can you be so sure?" Hanna argued and then he turned towards Ricky. "Sarge, what the fuck is going on?"

"I don't know, yet, but I'm going to find out," I heard Ricky say as I walked away.

I had two calls to make. My cousin and Terry, and I wasn't looking forward to doing either. I called Terry first.

"Terry, it's me, Frank. It's another rape. Yeah, you heard me. She's at the hospital being treated. Believe me, it's your jurisdiction."

I felt uneasy, this wasn't right. It was too deliberate and obviously personal. I called Jackie to check on her, "Baby, everything good?"

"Yeah, Frank." She was half asleep. "You okay?"

"Yeah, do me a favor. Check the front door, make sure I locked it."

"Why, Frank? There's nothing out here but deer."

"Just please check it anyway," I pleaded.

"Okay," Jackie said.

"I'll call you later, goodnight sweetie." I took a deep breath and left Ron's to go see the victim.

I met Terry outside the hospital. He was totally distraught. I walked up behind him. He didn't even flinch, yet he knew I was there, without looking. He started speaking, staring into thin air, "The girl in the hospital, she's an ex-dancer, Frank. She was an addict and I helped get her clean. She was doing very well. Do you know the chances of that?"

"I do." I was hesitant to say much. "How did it happen?" I asked.

"She doesn't remember or doesn't want to remember," Terry said in tears.

Then it dawned on me. Was this the woman he fell in love with, but who had a serious drug problem? One night at the bar, Terry had told me about a woman he'd loved and lost, all because of her addiction.

"Terry, was it Veronica?"

He just kept rambling, "She was so beautiful once." His voice shook. "Her face is half smashed and her womb was, was…" Terry broke down and cried uncontrollably. "Her insides were destroyed with something sharp."

I grabbed Terry and held him. I really didn't know what to do or say.

"Terry," I shook him. "Terry. Is there any physical evidence? Anything to tie this to someone?"

He yelled at me, "Hanna called me, Frank. 'BOO.' Fucking 'BOO.' You fucking know who did this."

I knew he was talking about Turner. But how the fuck was he going to prove it? Tommy never had camera systems at Ron's, for a variety of reasons. So that wouldn't be an option. No matter what we thought, our opinions were not enough to make an arrest, even less get a conviction.

To make matters worse, Terry did not look or sound right. He kept saying shit under his breath, some of it made no sense. The only words I heard were, "Boo, huh? Wait, bang is coming next. 'BANG' is coming next."

I got Terry back to his car and he went home. There was nothing from forensics to implicate Turner or anyone else for that matter. Veronica had bled out. She never recovered from her injuries. She was pronounced dead at the hospital.

*   *   *

Tommy:

I met my cousin Frank in the basement of our Grandfather's house, with Anthony.

"You guys wanna tell me why I had that girl bleeding out in my parking lot? I can't have messes like that at my front door. It's bad for business and worse, I don't need anyone looking at me as the culprit. *Capisce?*"

Frank had no answer for me. He knew if he speculated as to who did this, that he and Anthony would very quickly become an accessory to murder. And make no mistake, I would end the motherfucker who put that shit on my doorstep and I did not care if Frank and Anthony were cops.

So Frank just played it cool and said he didn't know.

"The victim died from her injuries, Tommy," Frank said. "She couldn't be questioned and there was no real evidence to pinpoint a specific person."

With Frank being virtually useless, I looked to Anthony, "You wanna tell me something?"

He just stared at me, then glanced at Frank, like he was doing me a fucking favor. "I don't know anything Tommy. It's not my case."

"Well, one of you better make it your business to make it your case."

"It doesn't work that way, Tommy," Frank said. "We don't get to choose our cases. We work for the police department, not for you."

"Are you really trying to piss me off, or what, Frank?"

"Tommy, I am not trying to piss you off. It's not our jurisdiction and I know you're upset."

"Upset?" Tommy said. "Upset? You don't know what upset is. Don't get me started Frank. Just do something."

ALLIANCE

Fed up with both Anthony and Frank, I walked up the stairs ranting and left, talking to myself.

*   *   *

Frank:

I looked at Anthony and he looked at me. We both suspected Turner was responsible for the rape and death of Veronica. And we both knew, if Tommy had his way, justice would be swiftly served and not in a courtroom.

"I don't care if it's Turner or anyone else for that matter," said Anthony. "I really don't. Tommy has his own ways of doing things. Let him handle it. We have more important things that need to get done than to worry about Tommy's business."

It was late and time to head home. When I arrived I found Jackie sound asleep. To be honest and I know it was a little selfish, but that's all I cared about, knowing that Jackie was safe under my roof.

I made myself a drink and went out to sit on the porch. It was a cool night and the moon was big and full. There was a bit of fog, which created a surreal, almost eerie atmosphere, like most fogs do. It was so quiet. I sat back in the chair and picked up the glass to take a sip when I heard a voice coming from behind me.

"Quite a night huh, Frank?"

I was so exhausted that I didn't even flinch. It was Turner, who had suddenly appeared out of nowhere and was now on my front porch. "Nice place, Frank. Looks like you and Jackie have settled in nicely. Playing house, I see?"

"What the fuck are you doing here?"

"Easy Frank, I'm on your side."

"My side?"

"I'm only just mildly angry, with you. But Terry, well, Terry is not my cup of tea at all."

I could have killed Turner right then and there and end whatever whacko game he was playing. However, I felt something else though. I couldn't explain it. I had this sickening feeling, like keeping him around could serve another purpose, whatever that might be. I know it sounds strange, but something else was going on here and I needed time to sort it all out.

"I heard all about that poor girl. She was so unlucky, Frank, especially after all that hard work to get herself out of the gutter. And with the help of your buddy, Flash, as well," Turner drawled, with a self-satisfied tone.

This fucking guy knew way too much about me and the people around me. What was he? A rapist? A murderer? What? All this was rushing through my head as he's speaking to me.

214

"Any clues who could have done such a thing?" he asked, playing dumb for sure, or at least I thought so at that moment.

"Get out of here Turner."

"Now, Frankie, ya know what they say and I mean they, just so we are clear. They say that girl screamed over and over for mercy. So disgusting isn't it? To damage the insides of a person like that? Whoever did that Frank, must be an animal. Or better yet, maybe just a misunderstood freak. You'd better be nice to me, Frank."

I just stared at him. I was angry and rattled. One thing I wasn't was unprepared. No matter how worried or even frightened I might have appeared to him, what he did not know was I was studying everything about him. No matter how distracted, a smart detective always begins to look for chinks in the armor of the person under investigation.

"Frank?" I heard Jackie call me and quickly switched gears, taking the focus off of what I had in front of me. "Frank?" she called out again.

"Well, I'll leave you be now Frank. By the way, you have a lovely home," he added as he slowly faded into the fog, just as quickly as he had emerged.

I just stared, watching him slip into the darkness and then I heard him for one last time.

"Oh, Frank, you really should lock this gate." He looked at me and said, "BOO," laughing wildly as he walked away.

THE BEGINNING

The next day I woke up sickened by that shithead's visit, yet knew it was best to keep it to myself right now. I couldn't put him away. I couldn't kill him. At least not yet, anyway. If he only knew how much of my cousin Tommy's blood ran through my veins, I could fall off that tight-rope any moment and that would be the end of Turner for good. And trust me, they would never find the body.

So I kept it to myself, for now. He knew where I lived and I knew where he was. I was prepared to do what was needed, especially if I had no choice. I was living a nightmare, obsessed with keeping Jackie safe and disciplined enough to know I had to handle this one way or another.

Weeks later I received a call from Jackie. She was working her regular shift as the bartender at Ron's bar.

"Frank, you need to come and get Terry out of here. He's had enough and he needs to leave."

I headed over there and there he was, drunk as could be. Jackie came over and I whispered to her, "You okay, baby?"

"Yes, but he's got to go," she said.

"What's he been doing?"

"You name it, everything from crying to breaking bottles, including giving me a marriage proposal."

Jackie looked me in the eye and could not help but laugh at the thought of Terry asking her to marry him. Of course, my immediate thought was that Jackie was giving me a hint, if you know what I mean. I smiled back at her and said, "Well, that's serious enough. I'll take it from here. Come on Terry, I'm taking you home."

"The hell you are," and he swung at me. I ducked and he fell forward. "I gotcha buddy." Terry was done and nearly out cold. "I'll take him home sweetheart. What time you leaving here?"

"In an hour," Jackie said.

"It's late, call me when you are headed out the door."

CHAPTER THIRTY-TWO

Jackie:

The bar was closing up and it was time to for me to leave. I was exhausted and getting sick of working as a bartender. But I knew we needed the money and I did not want Frank to work two jobs, so I was toughing it out until I finished school.

The parking lot was empty, just the help cleaning up inside the bar. I walked over to my car. I always parked it in a corner up against the grass, just short of the wooded area beyond. I went to get in the car when I heard a sound. It was like someone shuffling around in the high weeds. At first, I thought it was an animal, maybe a squirrel or a raccoon.

"Somebody there?" I called out. Then I saw a figure, a dark outline of a person. I called out again. "Hello?"

A voice emanated from the woods, "You work hard, don't you?"

"Huh? You're scaring me. What the hell are you doing here in the woods like that?"

"Just visiting."

"Well, there are better ways to do that."

"I left you something in your car."

I turned back towards my car and there was a rose on the seat. I turned back to look and he was gone as quickly as he'd appeared. At first, I was creeped out, but then I just figured he was probably drunk and being stupid.

* * *

Frank:

I dropped Terry off and brought him into his house, leaving him on the couch.

"Frank?" Terry mumbled.

"What?"

"He's following us, you know that right?"

"What do you mean?"

"You know what the fuck I mean. I saw him at the bar. He was sitting well behind me, Frank. He's not going away."

"What do you want to do about it? And don't fucking tell Jackie. I don't want her getting more creeped out than she already is."

"I have a plan," Terry slurred.

"A plan? You couldn't put two fucking sentences together a minute ago and now you have a plan?" I probably shouldn't have yelled at him like that, even though he'd asked Jackie to marry him twice. "Okay, so what's the fucking plan?"

"I'm gonna shadow him, I'm never gonna be that far behind him. The next time…" Terry paused for a second. "The next time, I'm gonna end this shit one way or another."

"Okay, Terry. Get some sleep."

Out of nowhere, he started screaming at me. "DON'T OKAY ME FRANK!"

I had to admit, I was a bit startled. I just looked at him and nodded. I knew what it meant but I was hoping he would be thinking more clearly tomorrow.

*　　*　　*

Jackie:

When Frank came home he found the rose I had inadvertently left on the kitchen table.

"You're getting flowers now?" he asked.

ALLIANCE

There was no way I was gonna mention that shit in the parking lot. I mean, what good could come from it? Besides, I deal with men like that all the time. They think they're impressing me. I would never do anything to hurt Frank and I should have just tossed the rose in the garbage when I had the opportunity.

"It was just my secret admirer, Frank," trying to laugh it off. "You know I was a dancer, Frank. People love me."

"Yes I do," Frank said. "But you don't have to be quite so popular."

He then grabbed me up in one of his bear hugs, before planting a big wet kiss on my lips. We both laughed, before dragging me off to bed.

CHAPTER THIRTY-THREE

Anthony;

I went by the bar to see Tommy so that I could report back on the events of the day. I was still doing his pickups and a few other errands.

I told Tommy, "The money was good and the drop offs were easy and legit."

"Anthony, you've been doing great for me," Tommy said. "But, I have a little problem. A delivery issue."

"Like what?" I asked.

"I need you to send a message with this next collection."

"Oh wait a minute, Tommy. I pick up and drop off your money and have no problem with that. But I'm not muscling anybody. That's crossing the line."

"I know, but I only need you to do this one favor for me. Just once."

"Why don't you send Benny?"

"I can't. There are reasons why he can't have a part in this. Besides, I don't want the guy dead. I just want you to smack him around a bit and Benny can't do that. With Benny, it's dead or nothing."

"Who is it?"

"He's that bum, Joe Morrissey."

"That piece of shit? He's harmless."

"He's also borrowed over 50K from me and now he has to pay up or else."

"How much?"

"I told you already. Just bring me back one of his fingers. I'll give you three thousand for the job. Anthony, it's the easiest money you will ever make."

"Hold on, wait just a minute. I thought you wanted him roughed up. There was nothing about cutting off body parts."

"That is roughed up to me. C'mon Anthony, just get it done."

"Okay, I'll take care of it."

"I knew I could count on you."

"Hey Tommy, it's just this one time. Don't forget that."

"Of course, Anthony, but of course."

*　　*　　*

Tommy:

I probably could have sent Benny to do this job, but I had more on my mind than just a simple beat down. I needed to reel Anthony in. The guy was on the edge of being an FBI agent and that meant a lot. I would now have Benny as my main hammer and on the other side of the fence, I would own a Fed.

Don't get me wrong, I loved Anthony like a brother and I pay him well for the little things he does for me. But, I would feel so much safer having his eyes on the Bureau. All I needed to do was get a little blood on his hands. You know, some incentive for him to stay loyal. Yeah, an obedient loyal soldier, who just happens to be an FBI agent. It doesn't get any better than that.

CHAPTER
THIRTY-FOUR

Frank:

Terry and I decided to partner up and do some surveillance work on Turner. We were just as sneaky as that little prick and it was our turn to watch him, instead of him watching us. Besides, I could keep a better eye on Terry too, making sure he didn't do anything stupid. Terry was slipping and I was getting worried about his mental state. Having him around allowed me to have a partner and it gave him something to do other than think about killing Turner.

So, we set up near Turner's apartment to see if we could establish his patterns. We could monitor when he came and went, places he frequented, shit like that. When you do surveillance work, it can be boring as well. In more cases than not, you wind up breaking each other's balls, just to pass the time. You can't help but fuck with each other a bit. So, Terry started it with some words about Jackie.

"You know Frank, I could have her if I wanted."

"Who, Terry?"

"Jackie. I could have her."

"Give me a fucking break, huh. If you could have, you would have her already you little shit."

"Hell, the way I dress, compared to you, I would have her in a minute. Why do you think they call me Flash? It's because I dress the part and get anything I want."

"You want me to put a good word in for you, Terry?"

"Ha, ha, very funny."

"Did you just laugh, Terry?

"Maybe I did, why?"

"I don't know. I just haven't seen you do that in a long time. Maybe you're turning the corner."

"What?" Terry said.

"Okay, too soon, maybe."

It suddenly got quiet in the car. But, after a few minutes, out of nowhere, Terry yelled out, "Okay, let's talk about the kid then, since you can't stop bringing him up."

I just looked away from him and realized that dead CI, that kid was never gonna leave him. As I turned to him to finally get into it, a radio call came in from his headquarters.

"Any unit in the area of Center Park, we have a report of a woman screaming."

We were a block away so we took it.

As we pulled up to the entrance of the park we had no idea who was involved, or what was going on. The park wasn't that big, but it did have some wooded areas and we would cover it quicker if we split up. There was nothing specific available about the exact location of the screams from dispatch, so we exited our vehicle and started to make our way through the park. It was dark and hard to see. As we were walking, the path split in separate directions.

"I'll go this way," Terry said, pointing to the path that went left.

"Well, then I guess I'll go to the right, fucker," I responded sarcastically. Of course, it had to be the darkest part of the park and I didn't have a flashlight.

"Okay asshole," Terry said. "Be careful. I would like to see you come back in one piece."

I echoed the sentiment to him, "You too, *amigo*," and away we went.

As Terry made his way in, he heard a woman scream. He grabbed his radio, putting it on a private frequency. It was better that way. Otherwise, you would hear unwanted traffic that could give your location away. Or worse, cut out any of our transmissions or requests for backup. The last thing we needed was a patrolman shooting his mouth off needlessly over the air while we were calling for help.

I should have known that Terry had no intention of letting me know about those screams. He was hell-bent on revenge and was not going to let me get in between him and Turner if that was who the cause of the screams turned out to be.

As Terry approached, he crept up behind a bush with his gun drawn. He then saw Turner with his pants down between his knees and he was straddled between a woman's legs. Turner had a small Billy club in his hand and was striking this woman repeatedly on different parts of her body as he was violating her. Every time Turner struck her, the woman screamed louder and louder, pleading for someone to come and help her.

"Shut up you cunt," Turner screamed, as he raised the club to hit her again. At that moment, Terry leaped from behind the bush and smacked Turner on the top of his head with the butt end of his gun.

"Down you go, you fuck," Terry yelled. "I got you, I finally got you."

It looked like Turner was knocked out. But in Terry's haste to render aid to the woman, he failed to handcuff him. It was a stupid mistake because while Terry was trying to stop the bleeding from the woman's wounds, Turner jumped up and struck him with the Billy club. The blow caused Terry's gun to fall to the ground, leaving him completely vulnerable.

228

"There you go, Flash," Turner gloated. "An eye for an eye!" He turned to flee, but couldn't resist taunting Terry. "Ha, ha Flash! Come and get me. Come and get me, Detective Robinson, if you can."

Terry shook off the cobwebs rendered from the blow, grabbed his gun and took up the chase after Turner.

It was at that point that I heard the woman shrieking, sounding almost like she was choking on her own blood. I finally located her and asked, "Are you alright ma'am?"

"Help me, please," she said and grabbed onto me.

I heard other units arriving, making their way through the park.

"Ma'am, which way did they go," I asked. "Ma'am?"

The woman pointed towards the southern section of the park.

"Look at me. You're going to be all right. My officers are right behind me and they will be here to help you right away." I could hear the officers getting closer.

"Over here," I yelled towards an approaching officer. "Take care of her. She needs medical assistance. Detective Robinson ran after the guy. Get additional units."

Terry was approaching the top of a hill crest. He had holstered his weapon and was exhausted from both the running and the hit he had sustained to his head. But, even as tired as he was, he was not giving up the chase and was closing in on Turner, who he now had in his sights. As he rounded the top of the hill, Turner slipped, giving Terry the edge he needed. With one last burst of speed, he jumped on Turner's back and they rolled down the hill into a wall of shrubbery.

When they landed, Turner turned and swung at Terry with the Billy club, missing. He laughed maniacally the whole time, while still struggling to catch his breath. Terry swung a wild leg kick that connected with Turner's knee. As Turner was going down, Terry hit him with a right cross.

"Down you go, you mother fucker," Terry screamed. "And down you better stay." Exhausted from the fight, Terry pulled his gun as Turner tried crawling away from him.

"Turn around, you fuck."

As Turner whirled around, Terry took aim and prepared to fire.

"Now you're gonna answer. Now I'm gonna end you."

Turner just looked at him and in that moment, for the first time in his life, he was scared of being killed. "Now easy Terry, let's just talk this over," Turner pleaded.

Terry grabbed at his head and screamed, "DON'T CALL ME TERRY!"

"Okay, okay," wailed Turner.

I had finally found them and could see their silhouettes in the reflecting light of the moon. I heard Terry yelling at Turner, "BOO mother fucker, BOO."

"Please, Terry. Come on… it was just a figure of speech."

As I got closer, I yelled Terry's name, but he paid me no mind. I saw the gun in his hand and it was pointed dead straight at Turner. I ran hard at him, hoping to stop him from making a grave mistake.

"I got a better word for you, you cocksucker," Terry replied. "BANG!" Terry pulled the trigger, but luckily, I was able to jar him just as he fired and the round went wide, sparing Turner's life. Turner was on the ground weeping like a child, just looking at me, with tears running down his face.

"Thanks, Detective. Thanks, Frank, thanks," he cried, as he was holding his head in his hands.

"What did you do?" Terry said to me, with a look that showed anguish for not having been able to end it with Turner.

Terry got his emotions under control and again pointed his weapon towards Turner. This time, I grabbed his hand.

"No, Terry, no," I implored.

"I've got to do this. Please, let me go. Let me finish him."

"No. You can't. You just can't."

"He ruined…" Terry said, not finishing his sentence.

"I know. I know what he did. I know! I really do. He hurt a lot of people and he's going to pay Terry. Let's put him where he belongs. Look at me, Terry. We will put him in a cage for a very long time, where all the other animals can feast on him."

By now, an army of other officers had shown up. I had Terry under control. He was slumped over and I was holding him up. His head was turned away from everyone. He did not want anyone to see him at his weakest moment. All I could say at that point was, "Place that fucker under arrest and get him out of here."

The patrolmen picked Turner up off the ground, handcuffed him and dragged him out of the park to a waiting marked unit.

Terry was still out of it, so I brought him back to his headquarters. Turner had been booked on multiple charges, in addition to the rape in the park. He was arraigned and remanded to jail on one million dollars bail.

CHAPTER THIRTY-FIVE

Frank:

The next day, I went to Terry's house. I had a key, so I let myself in. I found Terry in his bedroom, packing up his clothes like he was going on a trip.

"You going away?"

"Whatever gave you that idea?" he said in a hollow voice that made him sound like a defeated man. "Ya know Frankie, life is short. Too short."

Terry was rambling and I didn't really understand what he was talking about. He wouldn't even look at me as he spoke. He just kept looking down and packing his suitcase. "Ya know, I gave everything to this job. Everything. For what? For what? A man beats and rapes women and because he has money justice takes a pause."

"What are you talking about Terry? You got him and he's sitting in a jail cell now."

"Frankie, Frankie you never were one to stay up on things. And once again you are still trying to catch up on yesterday's news. What you don't know is that they bailed that mother fucker. He's out."

"That doesn't mean he's gonna get away with it Terry."

"I'm done, Frank. I'm really done. I'm putting my papers in. I'm retiring."

"What? Are you fucking crazy? What the fuck are you gonna do with yourself?"

Terry stopped what he was doing and gave me a hard look. "I am going to live Frank. I am going to laugh and try to enjoy what's left of my life. No more dead bodies, no more crying victims, and no more shitheads like Turner."

I was stunned. This was a reality check for me. Maybe it meant I should consider retiring myself, something I hadn't given much thought to. I just thought Terry and I would have gotten out at the same time.

*   *   *

It had been a long week and I was finally able to get home and was looking forward to getting some much-needed sleep. I was alone because Jackie was still at work and the house was peaceful. I was a light sleeper, it came with the job. As I was dozing off, I was startled by a noise outside. In the wake of having Turner visiting my house, I was a little paranoid when it came to strange sounds.

Grabbing my gun, I made my way out to the porch. I turned on the overhead light and saw that there was a package on the chair. When I opened it, I found a statue of a policeman. It had an engraving on it, "Number One Cop." There was also a card attached. It was from Turner and it simply said, "Thanks to you, Frankie, I'm baaaack."

Motherfucker! I should have let Terry kill that bastard. This was never going to end and he kept coming back to haunt me. To think, I didn't even know who this guy was and now, he was everywhere in my life. This was the last thing I needed. All I wanted to do was to live my life and enjoy the good things in it. Jackie and I were on the road to happiness and bliss. She had just finished school and gotten a job in a corporation, where she was going to work in the human resources department, starting shortly. We were solid and I couldn't imagine my life without her. So, my plan was to get her an engagement ring. I was at least gonna ask. Now, this motherfucker resurfaces looking to upset everything I was trying to build with Jackie.

*   *   *

Jackie:

"Tommy, I'm gonna close up, it's slow tonight."

"No problem, Jackie, go ahead and lock up."

Tommy left and I finished cleaning up the bar. When I was done, I went out the back door, bolted it and headed toward my car. As I got near where it was parked, I felt like I was punched in the stomach. On the hood was a rose, another red rose. I was scared. I should have told Frank about the first one that was in the car. I should have said something, maybe he could have done something about it. I heard a door slam behind me, then there was the voice, soft and melodic.

"I thought you liked flowers?" he asked.

"Uh, yeah, I do and thanks. What I don't like is you showing up here, uninvited."

"Easy, I was just trying to be nice. Show you how much I care."

I tried to get in the car so I could get away from this weirdo. But I couldn't help but say to him, "I'll tell you who's gonna care. My boyfriend, Frank, that's who. I would take a walk if I were you."

"Well, he's not here now. In fact, he's never around. You need someone better, someone, who will adore you."

Then he lunged at me and grabbed my hand. I was terrified, but I was not going to be a victim. I pulled away and yelled, "Get off! I'm telling you for the last time, leave me alone."

I jumped into my car and drove off, not looking back. I immediately called my sister.

"Hey, Jackie what are you doing?" said Tina when she picked up the phone.

236

ALLIANCE

"It happened again, Tina."

"What happened?"

"That crazy fucker showed up again in the parking lot."

"What did he want?"

"He keeps saying he's for me and he wants me, all that kind of shit. And he grabbed me. He scared the living shit out of me, Tina."

"Easy Jackie, you're safe now and you will be home soon. And not for nothing, but this guy isn't the first crazy person that's been attracted to you."

"I know, but this is different. This guy is creepy and I'm really freaked out."

"Well, maybe it's time to tell Frank."

"I don't know. I mean maybe it'll stop now. I don't want Frank doing anything crazy."

"Yeah, but I don't want anything happening to you either. If it happens again, I'm gonna tell Frank, myself."

CHAPTER THIRTY-SIX

Tommy:

I was at the Empire Diner in a meeting with Moe Browne, its owner, and Joe Knapp. I was investing in an auto repair shop located in the area called VinJ's. It was upstate, in a quiet little spot where nobody would find it and had an unassuming guy, by the name of Vinny Nuska, as its owner. I wanted to keep it quiet and away from all the greedy hands that were looking for a quick payday.

"Tommy, it's all set, sign this paper here and here and you are now in the auto repair business," Knapp assured me. I put my 'John Hancock' on the dotted line and the job was done. The only question was, what do I do with it now?

"There're two people manning the shop, Vinny and his brother Stephen. We'll need to determine what to do with them, but we can figure that out later," Knapp explained. He was always thinking ahead, that's why I liked that guy.

Anthony walked into the diner as Joe left.

"You got my bag for me?" I asked.

238

ALLIANCE

"Here you go, Tommy."

I opened it up and it looked right. Lately, I had been noticing the bag was a little light. I had been wondering if Anthony was getting too big for his britches and skimming a little off the top.

"Anthony, I want to make sure we are very clear on something."

"What's that?"

"When a bag is light, it starts a fight."

"I understand, Tommy."

"I love you Anthony, but don't ever cross me, ever. Don't ever forget business is business and personal is personal. I hope we are clear."

"Look, Tommy, I don't know where this is coming from, but okay. Besides, I have some good news for you. I got the job."

"What are you talking about now? Are you talking about the Fed gig?"

"You got it. I'm leaving the police department for the FBI."

"You are? Don't you think you are a little too old to be starting a new career? To be starting all over again?"

"Hey, I'm not that old and what's it to you anyway?"

"No matter. Well, Moe, let's drink us a toast to Agent Crespo, our new G-man."

"Hang on, Tommy. There's one other thing. I'm not Crespo anymore."

"What are you talking about, Anthony? You'll always be a Crespo."

"Yeah, but I had to change my last name."

"To what?"

"Cole. Anthony Cole. I'll never be Crespo again, so, get that out of your head!"

"Calm down, Anthony. I'm not mad at you. If you're happy, then I am happy. To Agent Anthony Cole. All the best my friend. Now can you pick up your fat ass and head down to The Saloon? When you're down there see Flatts and collect my package from him."

"No problem, boss. I'm on my way."

"And Anthony."

"What Tommy?"

"Don't change your name again on the way there, or Flatts won't know who the fuck you are." I looked at Anthony and broke up, laughing hysterically. He just stalked off and I could see he was pissed off.

Moe and I could not stop laughing. I said to Moe, "Maybe I'll change my name too, to Fucked!" I then fell off my chair, in tears, from laughing too much.

CHAPTER THIRTY-SEVEN

Frank:

With everything that had been happening, I thought it was time to have something good occur for a change, so I went to a jewelry store at a local mall, with Tina. We had been getting pretty close and I had grown fairly fond of her. She was a yoga instructor and from time to time, my therapist, in one form or another.

"So you wanna tell me what we are doing here, Frank?" asked Tina.

"Well, I'm gonna do it."

She looked at me, eyebrows raised, "Do what?"

"I'm gonna… I mean, I'm…"

"Frank stop stuttering, man. I don't have all day."

"I'm gonna ask your sister to marry me." I exhaled finally. "Is that okay, with you? I'm going to ask her to marry me."

Tina jumped into my arms, nearly knocking me over. If you didn't know better, the people around us thought I was asking her to marry me instead of Jackie.

"That's fantastic. I am so happy for the two of you. I could have picked so many other guys for her, but you will do."

"What?" I said, dumbfounded.

"I'm just kidding, Frank. Seriously, so what do you need me for?"

"Well, for one thing, she's always saying your hands are the same size as hers, so, I wanna try the ring on your hand first to see how it fits, plus I really want you to see what I picked out."

"Excuse me, ma'am," I said to the sales lady at the jewelry store. "Is my ring ready?"

She handed me the ring. It was white gold with a two-karat diamond, absolutely stunning in my humble opinion. But then, what did I know? That was why I needed Tina there. She would know best if Jackie would like the ring.

"Wow, Frank. She's going to love it. When are you doing this and where?"

"Well, you know how she loves the train station, so, I figured I would do it there. She sits there all the time and watches the trains come and go. Crazy right?"

"Yeah, about as crazy as you staring at the same bridge all the time," Tina said, joking with me. From time to time, I would go down to the park that overlooked the bridge and just stare out at the water.

"Ha, ha, very funny Tina."

"I'm just kidding Frank."

"Well, anyway, Friday she will be getting off the train coming back from her new job. Instead of waiting in the car for her, I'm going to be waiting for her on the platform. Then I'll walk her away from everyone and pop the question."

"You're so romantic Frank. A ring and a train station, you really know how to set the mood for a girl."

"What, Tina? No good? Should I be doing something else? I thought Jackie would love it."

"No Frank, actually for you two lovebirds, it's perfect."

So Friday arrived and I asked Paige Brown to do me a favor and videotape the proposal. I was nervous as all hell. We were so right for each other and it felt good. I was alive again, but I was apprehensive as well. What if Jackie said no? How was I gonna handle that? If she said no, did it mean that I'd misinterpreted the state of our relationship? That she didn't really love me? This is stupid. I had to stop making myself crazy. I needed to stay focused and follow the plan.

Jackie's train arrived right on time. I waited in the overhead walkway that connected the platform to the parking lot. I didn't want her to see me at first.

"Paige, you ready? Jackie's off the train and here she comes."

"Frank, will you shut up and stop the play by play. I can see her myself you know."

"Hey sweetheart," I said to Jackie, as I grabbed her arm to walk side by side with her. "How was your day?"

"It was okay, I'm just a bit tired."

"So, you're more tired than when you were dancing at all hours of the night?"

Jackie laughed. "No, I'm all right. And no, I'm not as tired as when I was dancing. I'm glad those days are behind me."

I reached a point on the walkway where I knew Paige had the best vantage point of Jackie and me. I stopped Jackie, stepped in front of her and looked into her eyes.

"Are you happy with me, I mean with us?" I asked her.

"Yes, yeah. Why are you asking Frank?"

"Well, I've been thinking. Um... uh..." I just couldn't get the words out and then Jackie interjected.

"Frank, what are you trying to say? What's wrong?"

"Jackie, oh fuck. Jackie, there's nothing wrong. I can't see myself with anyone else but you and I've never been this happy in my life." I reached into my pocket for the ring, which was Paige's cue to come out of hiding and start filming and taking pics. Jackie was a bit stunned to see Paige, but then looked back at me. I got down on one knee and took hold of Jackie's hand. I could see her face start to light up.

"Are you asking me to marry you?"

I nodded my head, yes. "Jackie, would you grow old with me and marry me?"

In true Jackie sarcastic humor, she answered, "Well... I have so much work to do. I'm just so busy, you know."

My mouth dropped open and I was a little in shock, fearing the worst. Seeing my sudden apprehension, Jackie burst out with a scream. "Of course I will marry you, you idiot." She jumped into my arms and I was never any happier in my life than at that moment.

We all walked away laughing and turning to Paige, I asked, "Did you get all that?"

"Yes, Frank. Stop worrying. I got it all and it was beautiful."

"I *am* worried. I just want proof, in case she changes her mind later on."

"You're an asshole, Frank. Come on, let's go celebrate," Paige declared.

Jackie was so excited she immediately called her sister to tell her the news.

"Yes, he did," I could hear Jackie telling Tina. "You knew? That's funny. I'll pick you up on the way to Grandma's house tomorrow and we can show her the ring. See you then."

Jackie said yes and it felt like the weight of the world was off my shoulders. It was a relief. We all decided to go to The Saloon to celebrate. When we got there, Tommy had candles lit and a special table set up for all of us to sit at. I have to admit the place had a real romantic feel to it. Flatts, Scopa, and Benny were already at the table and Tina had just walked in. We were being congratulated by everyone.

Anthony had shown up and went directly over to Tommy, where he handed off the bag as usual. I knew that some things will never change. But that was not going to tarnish the celebration.

"What are we celebrating?" Anthony asked.

Tommy responded, "Frank is getting married to this lovely ex-employee of mine."

"Wow, that's great news," Anthony said. "Congrats all around. I'm so happy for you guys."

Tina walked over to Tommy, which was rare since we all knew they did not really get along. From where I was sitting I heard Tina tell him, "Not bad, not bad at all, Tommy. I'm just a little surprised."

"Surprised? Surprised about what?" he responded.

"That you just let her go just like that. You usually don't let anything of value go, for free. So, yeah, I'm surprised."

"Uh, you know what Tina, it's a joyous event. Why don't you just drop it and have a drink."

Tommy raised his glass and made a toast. "*Salute*. To my cousin and to Jackie, long love and long life."

As we toasted, I turned my head to look around the room at everyone who had come to be with us. And then I saw him. He was moving slowly through the crowd. It was Turner. He had a hat on but wasn't really trying to disguise himself. He didn't say anything but walked right by me, he just nodded and smiled.

At that moment, I became concerned for Jackie. I hoped she wasn't paying attention enough to see Turner. I did not want this lunatic to ruin what was a perfect day. But I was relieved because when I saw her, she was showing off her ring to the girls at the bar. The reality was that Turner wasn't going away. But, at the same time, I was not going to let him terrorize my life. I watched him disappear into the crowd and then he was gone.

At the end of the night, I gave Tommy a big hug and thanked him for all he had done for us. Jackie and I went home. We were tired and got into bed right away.

"It was a great night, huh sweetie?" I said to Jackie as she turned out the light.

"Yes, baby. I am the happiest woman alive."

"Well, don't ever forget it."

We both laughed.

"What are you doing tomorrow?" I asked her, knowing she would be off from work.

"I'm gonna stop by Ron's to pick up a few things that I keep forgetting to bring home. Then, I'm going to my Grandma's house to show her the ring, with Tina. So, I'll be back a little late."

"Okay, no problem."

"I'll pick up some take-out on my way back, for dinner."

"You want me to bring anything home?"

"Nope, just you, Frank."

I laughed and it was one of the reasons why I loved Jackie. She was so real, there was nothing fake about her. Even when she had something on her mind, Jackie wasn't afraid to express herself.

"Frank, can I ask you something?"

"Sure anything, babe."

"If someone was bothering you, like more than normal, would you tell me?"

"Well, yeah, I would. I tell you everything, every day, anyway. Don't I?"

Jackie then got real quiet.

"Jackie, this is not about me listening and stuff is it? 'Cause if it is, I…"

"Stop, Frank, stop, alright? This is not about you. You're fine. I was just wondering, that's all, now get some sleep. I love you."

"I love you, too. Goodnight sweetheart."

CHAPTER
THIRTY-EIGHT

Frank:

I headed to work the next morning and went into the locker room, where I found Anthony cleaning out his locker.

"So, I guess it's time, huh?" I asked Anthony, knowing that he was off to the FBI.

"Well you knew it was coming Frank, didn't you?"

"I guess."

"And hey, you should be happy now. First, getting engaged to Jackie and now with me leaving, making *you* the best detective in the department."

"You're a funny guy, Anthony. Don't get carried away with yourself. You just became an agent and already you have an ego that overloads your ability."

"Yeah, yeah. Listen, I got to go. I'll catch up with you later."

"Okay, Agent Crespo."

"Cole, Frank. It's Cole."

"What? What is all that about? Agent Cole?" I looked at Anthony puzzled. Then it hit me, "So you actually changed your name, like you said you were going to do years ago?"

"Yeah, finally. Doesn't it have a nice ring to it? Never mind. Don't answer that."

Anthony started walking out of the locker room and then hesitated. He turned towards me, giving me a look, a sort of expression of longing. I swear he looked like he was never gonna see me again. Then he half smiled, saying, "Feels good to be free, Frank. Finally free."

*　　*　　*

Tommy:

I was proud of Frank. He had cleaned up, no longer a drunk and he looked good, too. Jackie had him in the gym, where he'd not only lost a few pounds, but he was really getting built. If I knew he would do it, I would take Frank on as my number one enforcer.

Anthony and Frankie weren't the only ones doing well. My businesses were flourishing, especially in Florida. In fact, I had a meeting scheduled in Miami at the end of the week. I was looking forward to it because any time I could expand my empire it meant my power base was extended as well. Not to mention, the extra cash didn't hurt. As I was contemplating the Miami move, Benny walked in with Scopa and Joe Knapp.

"Joe, everything set with my contact in Miami?"

"Yes, Tommy. Things are all arranged. When you get to the restaurant, there's a waitress named Angelina. She is blonde, very pretty and quite useful."

"Useful? What do you mean by useful?"

"You know, Tommy. She's the go-between for you. Angelina will meet you there. Introduce yourself and she'll bring you and Benny to our friend in Miami. And hey, Tommy, don't underestimate her just because she's good looking. Angelina can be deadly, too."

"Okay. I got it. Angelina is like a scorpion. One sting from that tail and it's curtains." I turned towards Scopa, "While I'm gone, I want you to hold things down here."

"No problem, boss. I got it covered. Enjoy the sunshine and watch out for scorpions," Scopa chuckled.

"Don't be a wise-ass. I don't need some bug to take the sting out of you."

It was a good thing our little meeting was breaking up, because in walked my favorite ex-dancer, Jackie.

ALLIANCE

"Well, well, look who came to visit," I said to Jackie and gave her a quick hug.

"Hey, Tommy. Thanks for putting together the party last night, it was great."

"You know, hiring you was the best thing I ever did. I don't know what he would have done without you. I can't tell you how many days Frank drove me and my friend Steve crazy talking about his divorce."

"Well, none of that stuff is ever easy, is it? But Frank is well worth the effort. He is a good man who was dealt a bad hand. And let's be honest Tommy, I give as much as I get, which is all good."

"Well, I wouldn't completely know, but I see your point. So what brings you here?"

"I left some clothes that I wanted back in the change room. I took the day off from work to try and do some errands, this being one of them. Then I'm going to my Grandmother's house with Tina to show her the ring."

"She must love that, Jackie. Those old folks, it's what they live for; to see the kids and the grandkids get married. The next thing you know, she'll be bugging you about having babies."

"I know Tommy. And believe it or not, Grandma actually likes Frank and that's not easy to get done. She's usually suspicious of everyone that comes into my life, but Frankie won her over."

"That's my cousin for ya. Listen, I gotta leave. I have a new bartender, Janelle, coming in about a half hour. Can you hold it down for me till then?"

"Sure, no problem. Anything for you, after what you did for us with the party and all."

"Oh and do yourself a favor, don't let Janelle read your palm. Life is better when it's a surprise."

"Ha, ha. Gotcha, Tommy. No palm readers today."

*   *   *

Jackie:

It was getting on in the day and this girl was already coming in late, even though she had just started working for Tommy. It was a bad sign for her, especially since Tommy did not put up with that kind of crap. Maybe he was getting a little soft. Then a guitar player named Danny Garrett came in. Everyone loved Danny. He played the blues like no one else.

"Jackie, isn't it?" Danny asked.

"Yes, that's me. What's up?"

"I thought you left here for greener pastures."

"Yeah, I did. But he's more Sicilian than green," I joked.

ALLIANCE

"Well, you know anyone with black hair and dark features looks better than most guys."

"That's funny, Danny. Who are we talking about, you or Frankie?"

"Hey, I put my time in with that boy. I told him it was his patriotic duty to get back to life, especially, after that divorce. Then you come, out of nowhere, cleaner than the Board of Health. He ate you up like the last supper. The boy fell hard. I'm happy for both of you."

"Well, thank you. I think."

"Anyway, it's getting dark out. These late winter days don't like sunlight. I'm just here to pick up my guitar. I'll be back tomorrow."

"Take care, Danny. It was good meeting you."

I started cleaning some of the glasses to kill time. Danny was right, it was getting late and I really did not want to be heading home in the dark. I knew it was going to be a late night. You know how it is with grandparents, once you're there, they never want you to leave. She always had to feed us first and then go over family history for the millionth time.

After what seemed like forever, Janelle finally came rushing in.

"I'm so sorry I'm late. It couldn't be helped. I couldn't find anything to wear and then I had to get my kid to my mother's. My life is a nightmare sometimes. I didn't mean for you to have to cover for me. But thanks anyway. I'm good now."

"It's all right," I said. "I totally get it. Life is hard and I would like to stay and chat, but I have to run."

I basically ran out the door. I was so late to get to my Grandmothers and I still had to stop and get my sister. I got into my car and figured I'd give Frank a quick call. It went straight to voicemail. I wanted him to know that I was delayed and not to worry.

"Frank, it's me. I'm running late. I wanted to leave you a message so you wouldn't worry. I just left Ron's and I am gonna get Tina and then head to Grandma's. I'll call you later. I love you."

I was making good time and was not that far away from Tina's house. Thankfully, there was no traffic. I stopped at a light and took a look to my left. Oh my God. It was him.

He was trying to say something. I put my window down and he shouted, "Please pull over! I need to speak with you."

I told him no. "What do you want from me?" I asked, getting irritated.

"Just pull over. Please. I want to talk to you, please, I need to."

I was scared to death. I was not going to stop and I could barely breathe. I stepped on the gas and sped away. I only had a few blocks to go. But he caught up to my car and was now pacing me. He started to box me in, leaving me less and less room in the lane, to drive. I tried to go faster to get away from him, but he kept chasing me.

Now I was beyond scared. I was hating myself for not telling Frank about this guy. I should have said something. Maybe Frank could have stopped him before it came to this. He was really closing in on me and was about to cut me off. As I tried reaching around for my phone, I looked at him and screamed, "Leave me alone you sick bastard! Get away from me. Why are you doing this?"

He cut in front of me and I tried to veer away from his car. He was pushing me toward the edge of the road and I kept going faster and faster in an effort to get away. I looked down and was able to grab my phone before I looked back at the road.

And then it happened.

My foot couldn't find the brake fast enough. I tried to navigate the turn in the road, but with the speed I was traveling, it was just too much and I lost control, hitting a utility pole head-on. The impact sounded like a bomb.

The front of the vehicle smashed right back to the firewall. In slow motion, I felt my head sail through the windshield as if I suddenly had the ability to fly. But, I was not thrown from the vehicle. Instead, my seatbelt kept me lodged in position as the vehicle collapsed around the rest of my body. I was stuck in that moment that everyone talks about.

I felt the life draining away from me, slowly and painfully. As I lay there, wedged in a part of the mangled wreckage, I saw him coming to the car. Maybe, just maybe, he was going to help. But he didn't. I could barely hear anything, my head was ringing. His fists were clenched and he was screaming at the sky. I thought about Tina and my Grandma. Would Grandma worry? I was probably late. I have to call her. I went to grab my cell phone, but instead, felt Frank's hand as he reached for me. We embraced, held on to each other, as I gazed into his eyes and I felt free. He looked and felt amazing. He hugged me and it was tight and warm, putting me at ease. He had a glow around him and it took my breath away. My lungs felt cold, I gasped a little, trying to make sense of what was going on.

Scenes of my life started flashing before me and I didn't know what was real but could feel a warm tear slide down my cheek. I tried to lift my hand to wipe it away, but every part of me was frozen. There was Frank again, he was glorious, I was so happy and at peace looking at him. Eventually, I succumbed to the comfort of that feeling and let go, giving my last breath to the world that had finally been so good to me.

*   *   *

"OH, MY GOD! She was so beautiful!" I screamed at the sky. Her car was split in two and an unrecognizable mangled mess. She was just as glorious in death as she was in life. "BUT WHY? It wasn't my fault." I said to nobody. This was all too much. I'd never felt this way before about anyone. She didn't have to die. It was an accident, right? I hovered over her lifeless body and realized 'You're not engaged and you are not getting married.' I reached into the car and grabbed that ridiculous trinket from her ring finger. Her skin was still soft and supple. I stared at her and took in her beauty.

Just then people were emerging from their homes to see what had happened. I heard sirens of the vehicles coming on the scene and knew I only had a few last seconds to stare at her. Turning away from Jackie's car, I shoved the ring in my pocket, before looking back at her for one last time. Her eyes were wide open staring at me. I thought to myself, 'You deserved better, you deserved everything I just took from you. If you can't have any of those things, why should anybody else?'

THE END

(To be continued…)

Acknowledgements

The authors would like to thank those who made these characters come to life. In particular, we would like to recognize the following actors and actresses for putting their best faces forward: Liz Abreu, Robert Ardisi, Salvatore J. Ardisi, Chris Bartolini, Tommy Bartolini, Tina Bellino, Joan Caluori, Rob Caluori, Jr., Rob Caporale, Evan A. DeMarzo, Lance DeMarzo, Janelle Dwyer, Jay Donnarumma, Trevor Elmo, Brian T. Fiorio, Colum Flattery, Chris Laird, Christina Lang, Grant Lang, Adam Monaim, Bobby O'Neill, Sr., Angelina Perevozchikova, Myo Perez, Ricky "Rockstar" Perez, Keith Preston, Miguel Rojas, Wilbert Ross, Angel "Rocky" Sepúlveda, Seamus Skeffington, and Donald Tucciariello. And a special thanks: Tony Welch, George Strelakos, Jr., Neal Alpuche, Dave Wenger, Arn El (Maui) Malabanan, Vincent Januska, Sr., Stephen Januska, Randy Lavello, Victoria, Trish, Breanne, Shanna, Nicole, Vincent Januska, Brian David, Ramone Perez, Jasmin Barajas, Julia, Justin, Fran Ardisi, and Debbie Ardisi.

We would like to thank the following locations where Alliance, the webseries, was filmed:
Anthony's Coal Fired Pizza, White Plains, NY
Brazen Fox, White Plains, NY
Central Park, New York City, NY
The Confidante Hotel, Miami Beach, FL
Empire Diner, Monroe, NY
Finnegan's Way, Miami, FL
Lazy Boy Saloon, White Plains, NY
Pierson Park, Tarrytown, NY
Public House, Pelham, NY
The Rittenhouse, Philadelphia, PA
Ron Blacks Beer Hall, White Plains, NY
Vin-J's Oil & Lube, Chester, NY

alliance

THE FRACTURE

Book 2

Frank:

Sleeping peacefully was something I was getting used to. Why not? Life could not have been better. I was in love again and with a girl who made me feel whole. Even in my dreams, there was bliss. As images of Jackie swirled in my head, I could hear her calling, 'Frank, come here. Look how beautiful of a day it is. The sun is shining and the sky is so blue.'

I watched Jackie dance in the grass, with Long Island Sound in the background. The water looked like a sheet of glass, with Jackie's reflection shining from it. She looked like an angel and the shimmer of the water provided a magical glow to her silhouette. But there was something else going on as well and I could hear myself calling out to her, 'Jackie, watch what you're doing, you're getting close to the rocks.'

Jackie was twirling around in joy, oblivious to her surroundings. I noticed she was getting dangerously close to the rocks that dotted the shoreline. In my dream, I called out, 'If you fall on them, you'll take quite a scraping on the way down from the jagged rocks. Jackie, you're too close.'

Then my cell phone rang. I could hear Jackie saying, 'Stop being a party-pooper, Frank. Answer your phone.' I looked at the phone and it just rang and rang. I tried to pick it up but I couldn't feel it in my hands. I looked up at Jackie. Something was wrong because she was fading away, while the phone kept ringing continuously. I couldn't see Jackie anymore and I slapped at the phone, still unable to touch it. I felt anger and frustration. I smacked at the phone harder and harder. Then, I woke up.

"What the fuck?" I nearly fell out of the bed. Looking at the time, I noted it was only 9:30 p.m. I must have dozed off. I checked my phone and noticed I had a missed call from Ricky Rosa. He had sent me a text, as well.

The message read:

'Frank, call me ASAP, 911. It's very important.'

* * *

Made in the USA
Middletown, DE
10 November 2018